Praise for
a proud
achievement
and
a master novelist—

LAST REVEILLE

and
DAVID MORRELL

"A moving account of hard men in
a hard land."
—*Hartford Courant*

ooooooooo

more . . .

"A tale of survival and cunning set against a vivid panorama of scorching desert and dusty desolation ... a good, fast read.... A thoroughly unpredictable finale rewards the reader right down to the last sentence of the book."
—Edmond G. Addeo, co-author of *Midnight Special*

ooooooooo

"A strong, well-written novel ... Morrell gives us vivid, moving pictures ... one has the feeling of being there."
—*Weekender*

ooooooooo

"As graphic as a glass-plate photograph."
—*Kirkus Reviews*

Also by David Morrell

Fiction
First Blood (1972)
Testament (1975)*
Last Reveille (1977)
The Totem (1979)
Blood Oath (1982)
The Hundred-Year Christmas (1983)†
The Brotherhood of the Rose (1984)
Rambo (First Blood Part II) (1985)
The Fraternity of the Stone (1985)
The League of Night and Fog (1987)
Rambo III (1988)
The Fifth Profession (1990)*
The Covenant of the Flame (1991)*
Assumed Identity (1993)
Nonfiction
John Barth: An Introduction (1976)
Fireflies (1988)

†*Limited edition. With illustrations by R. J. Krupowicz.*
Donald M. Grant, Publisher, West Kingston, Rhode Island.

*Published by
WARNER BOOKS

DAVID MORRELL

LAST REVEILLE

WARNER BOOKS

A Time Warner Company

This book is history. While several characters and incidents have been invented, the substance of this book is based on fact. Wherever possible, the author has used actual dialogue and details from the events depicted.

The dispatches in Chapters 1, 2, and 3 are from *The New York Times*, March 9, 1916, the speech in Chapter 17 from *The New York Times*, March 15, 1916. © 1916 by The New York Times Company. Reprinted by permission.

The quotations in Chapters 10 and 46 are respectively—somewhat altered and condensed—from Clarence Clendenen: THE UNITED STATES AND PANCHO VILLA (© 1961 by the American Historical Association. Used by permission of Cornell University Press); and from Robert Leckie: THE WARS OF AMERICA (Harper and Row, 1968).

WARNER BOOKS EDITION

Cover design by Jackie Merri Meyer
Cover photograph by Don Banks
Hand lettering by Carl Dellacroce

This Warner Books Edition is published by arrangement with the author.

Warner Books, Inc.
1271 Avenue of the Americas
New York, NY 10020

W A Time Warner Company

Printed in the United States of America

First Warner Books Printing: June, 1994

10 9 8 7 6 5 4 3 2 1

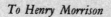

To Henry Morrison

War is cruelty, and you cannot refine it.

—WILLIAM TECUMSEH SHERMAN

Introduction

Last Reveille, my third novel, was originally published in 1977. I had already written *First Blood* (1972) and *Testament* (1975), two drastically different approaches to action, and now I wanted to explore action in another way— through the perspective of history. Any reader familiar with my later international thrillers—*The Fraternity of the Stone* (1985) and *The Fifth Profession* (1990), for example—is aware of how important history is to the contemporary settings of those narratives. But back in the mid-1970s, I hadn't yet indulged my fascination with the past.

In retrospect, it isn't surprising that history would so occupy my imagination. After all, in 1970 I received my doctorate from the Pennsylvania State University and subsequently became a professor at the University of Iowa. My specialty was American literature, and my approach was in the spirit of what is these days called New Historicism, the interpretation of a literary work by placing it thoroughly in its historical context. Still, being fascinated with history is one thing; finding a way to use it as the basis for an action novel is quite another.

As things turned out, an alternate passion of mine—film—showed me the way. Because my fiction aims to be vivid, I'm often asked if I have movies in mind when I set out to write a book. That's a complicated question. For certain, I have never chosen a subject or developed a plot or used a technique merely because I thought it would make a novel easier to sell to a film company. On the contrary, I fear that a book suffers when its author has a Hollywood perspective.

But film has nonetheless influenced me in various ways. I wouldn't have set out to be a writer if, as an impressionable teenager, I hadn't fallen under the spell of a television show, *Route 66* (1960–64), about two young men in a Corvette who search for America and for themselves. As much as I liked the lead actors, Martin Milner and George Maharis, I was even more impressed by the words they spoke, the adventures they experienced, and the meaning they took from those adventures. I began to notice a name in the credits of almost every show: Stirling Silliphant, the man who co-created and wrote most of the episodes. I suddenly knew that I wanted to be what Stirling Silliphant was—a writer. Stirling Silliphant eventually became my mentor, and in a wonderful closing of a circle, he was the executive producer of the 1989 miniseries that NBC adapted from my novel *The Brotherhood of the Rose* (1984). To this day, I'm compelled to explore the blend of action and introspection that attracted me to Stirling's work. No novel influenced me more than his scripts.

One particular film, not by him, also had a long-lasting effect on me, and it has particular application to *Last Reveille*. In 1969, the first day it opened, I went to see Sam Peckinpah's *The Wild Bunch* and was overwhelmed.

Peckinpah's end-of-the-west story of an aging band of American outlaws who flee a posse and try to cling to their old ways in 1916 Mexico stunned me with its brilliant images and complex approach to violence. I became interested in the film's historical setting and eventually focused on an event that is only slightly referred to in the movie—"Black Jack" Pershing's expedition into Mexico in pursuit of the bandit Pancho Villa.

On March 9, 1916, Villa and his men had snuck into the United States and staged a bloody predawn raid on the small New Mexico border town of Columbus, subsequently fleeing back into Mexico. In retaliation, the U.S. government had ordered a large military force to go after him. In effect, the United States was invading Mexico. Simultaneously, World War I was ravaging Europe. America had not yet entered the war, but there were rumors that Pershing's so-called punitive expedition was a dress rehearsal, that America's foray into Mexico had less to do with Pancho Villa than with the necessity of training a considerable number of American soldiers for overseas combat. At the time, the U.S. military was underequipped and understaffed, accustomed to tactics from the nineteenth century. Suddenly it had to absorb tens of thousands of recruits and become expert in modern warfare. In one of those richly suggestive watersheds of history, the old and the new were dramatically juxtaposed, soldiers on horseback riding next to cars and trucks while airplanes flew overhead.

America's military entry into the modern age resulted in a corresponding loss of innocence, and the more I considered the implications, the more determined I became to write a novel that dramatized the unique suggestive events that occurred in 1916 in Mexico. I read everything I could about Pershing and his expedition. I went to Columbus, New Mexico, still a small town whose old buildings eerily evoke 1916, and in the midst of a dust storm walked the route of Villa's attack. I studied countless sepia-tinted photographs of the period. Finally, I felt that I had immersed myself sufficiently to dramatize the feeling of the facts.

But I'm not a historian—I'm a novelist. No matter how much research I had done, it meant nothing without a story, a very personal, very human narrative that needed to be played out against the powerful historical forces that Pershing and Villa represented. One obvious possibility was to make Pershing and Villa the main characters of the novel. But the notion of stepping beyond history to invent thoughts and emotions for actual persons made me uncomfortable. Instead, I wanted the freedom to imagine; the main characters had to be entirely my own. But who would they be? Again my inspiration came from the movies.

On occasion, a unique film actor has a long enough career that audiences construct a gestalt of all the actor's roles and impose that gestalt on the most recent role that the actor has played. In that way, the current role gains from the accumulation of other roles that the actor has played. Gregory Peck, James Stewart, Cary Grant—these are a few of those whose charisma and longevity have caused audiences to associate their present performances with a host of fondly remembered past ones.

Another actor whose long career gained from this phenomenon was John Wayne. When he received an Academy Award for his performance in *True Grit* (1969), many commentators felt that the award was not so much for that particular film as for the best of Wayne's other work, *Stagecoach* (1939), *Red River* (1948), *She Wore a Yellow Ribbon* (1949), and *The Searchers* (1956), to name a few. In sequence, these films showed him aging. Many were *about* aging. The young gunfighter of *Stagecoach* had become the about-to-retire cavalry officer of *She Wore a Yellow Ribbon*, who in turn became the crotchety old marshal of *True Grit*. The protagonists in *Red River* and *The Searchers* had been crotchety as well, to put it charitably— one is psychotic, the other a racist—and the memory of them added depth to *True Grit*'s lighter, humorous character. A few years later, Wayne played an aging trail driver in *The Cowboys* (1972), and that trail driver gained by association with Wayne's determined, afraid-to-get-old trail driver in *Red River*.

In his final film, *The Shootist* (1976), life and fiction vied bitterly, for Wayne played a character who was dying from cancer, as the actor himself would in 1979. That film was released one year before *Last Reveille* was published. I was halfway through the novel by then, and as a consequence, the movie had virtually no influence on me. With one exception. At the start of *The Shootist*, director Don Siegel skillfully inserted film clips from many of Wayne's previous westerns, creating the pretense that Wayne had been the same character in all of them, showing that amalgamated character as he grew older. The technique dramatized the phenomenon I described above, and it reinforced in me a decision that I had made when I started composing *Last Reveille* in 1975.

The decision has to do with perspective. I've referred to the 1916 events in Mexico as a historical watershed. After Pershing modernized the U.S. military, for example, he led his soldiers to Europe and World War I. George S. Patton, Jr., a lieutenant who gained battle experience with Pershing in Mexico, went on to become one of America's most important commanders in World War II. In those cases, the movement of events was forward. But a watershed implies a movement in the opposite direction as well, and for my purposes, that movement was backward, into the past.

To me, the military events in 1916 in Mexico could be understood only by comparison with America's immediately previous military experiences in Cuba (1898) and the Philippines (1899–1902, with sporadic later incidents). But why stop there? The earlier wars against the American Indians had tactical relevance to Pershing's war against Villa. And the Civil War (1861–65) had relevance to the Indian Wars. The ruthless marauding tactics that the North used to defeat the South were later used against the Indians. For that matter, the same commanders, Sherman and Sheridan, designed both brutal campaigns.

What if one character, a fictionalized John Wayne, could represent America's military history from the middle of the nineteenth century up to 1916? At age sixty-five, he would be old enough to have participated as a youth in the Civil War. He would have been in the Indian Wars, in Cuba, in the Philippines. Now he's with Pershing in Mexico. But he knows he won't be allowed to go overseas to the First World War. Seeing planes fly overhead, he realizes that his way of life is over. Still, for his own private complex reasons, he doesn't want to let the old ways die, so he agrees when a frightened young recruit badgers him for lessons in how to stay alive.

Unable to resist the allegory, I called the older man

Miles Calendar because of the implications of space and time. The recruit's name, too, has allegorical significance: Prentice. Put ''ap'' before that name, and you have a perfect description of what the boy is. Amid the chaotic and brutal search for Villa, Calendar teaches Prentice by means of lengthy stories that evoke the past. In the process, the two form a powerful emotional bond, but that is abruptly destroyed when Prentice loses his innocence just as America loses more of *its* innocence.

Given the scope of these themes, this book could have been a thousand pages long. But from the start, I resisted the impulse. Researching the punitive expedition, I had been struck by the stark tone of the eyewitness documents. Visiting Columbus, I had been mesmerized by the impressive sparseness of the desert. Studying page after page of those sepia-tinted photographs, I had been captivated by the primitive simplicity of the decades-old images. It seemed to me that my prose ought to match the hard-edged leanness of my sources. I hoped that the reader would feel a pressure of compression, a weight of implication beneath the austere narrative.

The chapters are unusually short, even for me—they are intended to be like a series of old photographs. Sentences often have a number of participial phrases—those ''ing'' words are intended to communicate the book's historical theme by suggesting a welter of accumulating action. On occasion, the action stops while the narrator comes forward to explain a historical detail or to introduce a passage from a history book—the device is intended to break the division between past and present. The dialogue tries to accomplish the same purpose, for exchanges that sound contemporary have frequently been taken from transcriptions of what was actually said back then. Whenever possible, I did not invent. To an unusual degree, not only major plot devices but minuscule details have a basis in fact.

In a broad sense, all of my novels have been thrillers, inasmuch as they deal with visceral action. But within that category, I've written many different kinds: the nihilistic thriller (*Testament* 1975), the nonsupernatural horror thriller (*The Totem* 1979), the international thriller (*The League of Night and Fog* 1987), and the ecological thriller (*The Covenant of the Flame* 1991). *Last Reveille* is my historical thriller, one of the most unusual books that I've written, and one of my favorites.

ONE

1

El Paso, Texas, March 8

(Special from The New York Times*)*
Unconfirmed reports received today by General Gabriel Gavira at Juárez indicate that two Americans named Franklin and Wright were killed by Villa bandits Monday at Pacheco, between Casas Grandes and Janos, Chihuahua.

The advices contained nothing as to the fate of the wife and small son of Mr. Wright, who were reported with the men at Pacheco.

Gavira declared the men, said to be Mormon ranchers living west of Casas Grandes, disregarded warnings he had sent to all American residents of northwest Chihuahua when he first learned of Villa's movements in that region.

2

COLUMBUS, NEW MEXICO, MARCH 8
Francisco Villa and his forces today reached the ranch of the Palomas Land and Cattle Company at Nogales, Chihuahua, ten miles below the border and forty-five miles east of here, according to a telegram sent by the American foreman of the ranch which was received here today.

The message made no mention of Arthur McKinney, James Corbett, and James O'Neill, American cattlemen believed to have been taken prisoner yesterday.

3

WASHINGTON, MARCH 8
What was regarded as confirmation of the report that Villa was on Palomas ranch, a few miles south of Columbus, New Mexico, was received today by the State Department. No information

*reached Washington concerning the report that
Villa killed two Americans named Franklin and
Wright between Casas Grandes and Janos. All the
Americans employed on the Palomas ranch except
one were reported to have crossed to the American
side on the approach of Villa, who was said to
have with him about four hundred men.*

□□□□□ 4 □□□□□

COLUMBUS, NEW MEXICO, 1916
There weren't even any trees.

There was some scrub brush in among the tents and
buildings, some thick reeds along the ditch that ran beside
the north–south road through town, scattered tumbleweed
and cactus, a desert full of rock and sand.

He couldn't quite believe it. Looking out the window,
he had thought that this must be the outskirts. Then the
train had stopped, and he had stood up with the others,
shouldering his knapsack, stepping down, and outskirts,
hell, he looked up past the engine where the buildings
ended, and the whole town wasn't more than four blocks
wide. He stood there trying to adjust to it.

El Paso had been green, the Rio Grande, the electric
trolley. For his three days there, he'd spent his spare time
sitting in the Fort Bliss square, cooling off beneath the
wind-blown trees. Up north where he had come from, it

was still winter, the trees still bare, the grass still brown, but March in Texas was a good time, warm enough with spring rain to bring out color, not yet hot enough to wilt and pale. They had told him of the desert flowers in spring, but once outside El Paso there had been no flowers, and he had wondered why the other soldiers looked with amusement at him, and now he knew. There wasn't anything. Adobe shacks, frame houses, hard-baked streets, a dog, lean-flanked, tongue hanging, disappearing in the ditch. He looked down at the sun-cracked timbers of the railway platform, squinted at the dust that filled them, dragged his boot across them, squinted at the dust-filmed windows of the station, licked his lips, and took another look.

As much as he could tell, this side of town was camp. The soldiers he had been with on the train had gone off to the left, coming back from leave, carrying their knapsacks toward a string of long, narrow wooden buildings, barracks likely, horses neighing from in back of them. He walked down to the far end of the platform and saw a flag and a sign CAMP FURLONG and two officers coming from a squat adobe building. The sun was in his eyes, well down toward the tracks, the sky still white and hazy, and with his heavy woolen shirt sticking to his sweaty chest, he turned to face the train, the engine sounding louder now, cars moving, the last one chugging past. It must have been the angle of the sun, because the other side of town was much the same, more frame shacks, adobe buildings, a few two-story structures that looked like they were hotels maybe, a store, a post office, the same hard gritty streets, but they were tinted brown now from the sun, and strangely different, soft and somehow distanced, as in photographs.

He saw two men in shapeless suits go around a corner, heard an automobile approaching from the north, walked to the edge of the platform, and looked up toward the sound but couldn't see the car although the road ran straight that way and he could see the upper end of town. Five blocks. No water in the ditch. There wasn't anything.

□□□□□ 5 □□□□□

THE sergeant must have been there all along, staring at him through the dust-filmed windows of the station. Now he heard the dry creak of the door behind, and turning saw the sergeant standing in the doorway, stark-faced, sleeves rolled up, short-bodied, heavy-hipped, loose olive shirt and baggy breeches tucked in to the boots.

Intimidated, he stiffened to attention and saluted.

"What's your name?" the sergeant demanded.

"Prentice."

"Prentice, *Sergeant*. And there's no need to salute. Let's see your orders."

He fumbled in his knapsack and produced them.

"What about the rest of you?"

"I don't know what you mean."

"The rest of you. We asked for ten, they gave us three, so where's the other two?"

"I really just don't know."

"This says you're from Ohio. Nineteen. Six weeks in

7

the service, and they put you in the cavalry.'' The sergeant stopped and shook his head. "The cavalry. I don't know what this place is coming to. So all right what about them?"

"I don't understand."

"Horses. What about them? What kind do we use?"

"Oh, *I see*. *That*."

"Yes, that's right. *That*. So what about them? Now you're in the cavalry, so prove it. What about the—"

"Cross between Arabian and quarter."

The sergeant blinked and then continued. "What about the saddle?"

"Modified McClellan."

"What's it mean?"

"An open slot between the pommel and the horse's back. No saddle horn. A high front and a rounded cantle."

"Any good?"

"A little but not much. Rifle scabbards slip. The two side pieces sink, the pommel touches, and the spine takes all the load. Besides, the stirrup leather is too heavy. It wears against the horse's hide."

"Where'd you learn all that? Some polo club in Cincinnati?"

"No. Near Cleveland. On my father's farm."

The sergeant pursed his lips and stared at him. "Well, maybe they were right to send you after all."

THE barracks was ten feet square, three up-and-down bunks, some shelves, a small potbelly stove, pinups from Sears catalog—women's girdles—on the walls.

"This'll do until tomorrow," the sergeant said. "These men are all on leave."

Prentice set his knapsack down and looked around. The floor was dirt. The walls were boards with cracks between that showed the setting sun. He looked—each bunk leg was inside an open can. He turned to face the sergeant, and he frowned.

"Sure, and while you're at it, notice that the bunks don't touch the walls."

Prentice didn't understand.

"Three things you should know about. This isn't like up north. Spiders, snakes, and scorpions."

The thought of spiders made Prentice hunch.

"The first thing you come in here, take this broom and poke it underneath the bed." The sergeant showed him how to do it. "Then you pull the covers back and make sure no surprises are in there. In the morning, poke beneath the bed again. Shake your clothes and dump your boots and put them on real slow. There's nothing to it once you get the gist."

"What about the bunk legs in those cans?"

"A quarter full of kerosene."

The sharp sweet smell was everywhere.

"If something wants to crawl up on you while you're sleeping, it's got to pass the kerosene. It never does. Fill up one of these, and in a week you'd be surprised the things you find."

Prentice didn't want to think about it.

"Well, that mostly does it. Tell the cooks you're new and get a meal. I'll see you in the morning. Where'd you say that farm was?"

"Outside Cleveland."

"Yeah, I'm from up near there myself. Remember what I said about the boots." And the sergeant was gone.

Prentice stood in the middle of the room, smelling the kerosene, staring at the slats of sunset on the floor, smelling the dust and splintered wood, and, in a moment, breathing slowly, he licked his lips to swallow. He didn't move for quite a while. Then he took his round-brimmed trooper's hat and hung it on a peg, wondered where he ought to put his knapsack, cinched it tight and hung it on another peg, walked to the open door and the sergeant wasn't anywhere. Prentice looked out at a string of shacks across from him, the barracks farther over, soldiers sitting on the stoop, a cloud of swirling dust from over where he guessed the stables were. A two-horse buckboard clattered past the barracks, the soldiers on the stoop not even looking at it. Then the light changed and the sun was gone. The air got cold. A wind came up. Prentice stood at the open door, wondering if he should eat, thought of bacon, coffee, hardtack, and his mouth went sour at the thought of it; looked over by the beds, looked out again, and closed the door.

☐☐☐☐☐ 7 ☐☐☐☐☐

THE thunder woke him.

He was dreaming of green fields and blossoming orchards, running up a slope, his father by an oak tree up there, and the more he ran the farther up the top became, his father just a blur by now, and then he got there, stumbling, and his father wasn't there. He swung full circle, looking for him, staring at the long green fields, the growing grass, and one long hill with rocks at one end seemed to him a grave, his father in there straining at it, struggling to burst through, and then the rain began, soft at first, then gusting at him, lashing. He couldn't see. He reached out to touch the tree but couldn't find it, stiffened in the sudden lightning and the thunder.

They were directly outside the door, and he was sitting up in bed, his arms outstretched, uncertain where he was. The sergeant had been wrong. Only one man from the shack had gone on leave. The others had come in shortly after nine and said hello and gone to sleep, and now they threw off covers, saying, "Christ Almighty! What the hell is happening?"

The gunfire settled any question. The walls shook from the constant thunder, and the troopers scrambled from their beds, slipping on their breeches, grabbing rifles, reaching for the door, and ran out into the darkness.

Meanwhile Prentice hadn't moved. From where he sat, he saw the swirling images of chaos passing out there. More gunfire, flashes lighting up the night. Before he knew, he'd put on trousers where he'd set them folded on the bed, reached for boots, froze as he remembered what the sergeant had told him, left them, and stumbled puzzled toward the door.

It seemed there were horsemen everywhere. An endless roaring crush of them, massive objects crashing past. There was gunfire from the buildings, horsemen dropping. Flames, one shack on fire, another starting, hard to tell in the dust from the horses and the gloom, but in the cracking muzzle flashes from the riders' handguns, it looked like they were Mexican, their dark grim mustached faces rimmed by their sombreros, bandoleers across their chests, voices shrieking, eyes aglare.

He didn't even know when he had done it. One moment he was standing, half asleep and stunned by what was happening, his hand outstretched on the grainy doorjamb. The next thing he was walking slowly forward, hypnotized by what was going on around him, ready to be swallowed. He couldn't stop himself. The horses were around him, closer, larger, swirling on both sides of him, and he knew he shouldn't be there, told himself to run, but couldn't make himself. The flank of one horse struck and spun and almost dropped him, his arms outstretched to catch his balance, falling to one knee. He braced himself and stood and saw another rider coming down on him, machete raised to strike. Thirty feet, then twenty, larger as it came. He felt the soft flesh on his neck and chest where the blade was going to strike, told himself to run but couldn't, the horseman even closer, larger, machete arcing, as a muzzle flashed from somewhere to his left and punched the rider from his horse, foot catching in the stirrup, horse breaking stride and swerving, charging past, the rider, foot still in the stirrup, bouncing, twisting, as he passed.

Prentice couldn't breathe. He told himself he had to breathe. He turned in stupefaction toward the shot, and there was nothing. He stared to penetrate the darkness.

Nothing.

And then a piece of the darkness detached itself. Powerful and massive. A man, tall, square-faced, barrel-chested, a civilian, was running, crouching, firing, running. He had a semiautomatic pistol in one hand, the hand that he was firing with, and a lever-action rifle in the other, and he was rushing toward Prentice as the rider had. Prentice stood there stunned, everything the same as with the rider, except that this time there was no shot to drop the man as he came charging up and shouldered Prentice so hard they both went crashing.

Prentice's mouth twisted in the dirt. "What is it? Who the—"

"Dammit, you stay down!"

Prentice felt a hand on his belt, another on his collar, dragging, cursing, lunging him. He saw the shack loom up before him, felt the two hands thrust him in upon the floor.

And then as fast as he had come, the civilian was whirling in the darkness, pausing in the flashes from the riders' handguns, shooting twice at them. Then bolting off in their direction, he was gone.

Prentice lay there on the dirt floor of the shack, staring out the open doorway in the man's direction. He felt the pressure on his spine and neck where the man had grabbed at him, felt the scratches on his knees and hands where he had dropped. And something else, something in his hands. The lever-action rifle. He hadn't even known the man had left it. Prentice stared at it, surprised to find that he was moving, working it, raising it, not really aiming as he fired once out the doorway at the rush.

□□□□□ 8 □□□□□

THE rider took it in the neck and toppled. The civilian fired again and hit another in the chest. He was big, six feet three at least but maybe more, his high-peaked, up-brimmed cowman's hat making him seem even taller. He was large-faced, thick-necked, heavy-shouldered, the muscles of his arms and chest bulking underneath his shirt and vest. Long and solid legs, massive torso, the wonder was that he had moved so fast and smoothly, running from the darkness. The second wonder was that he had moved with any speed at all. Because as he had crashed down on Prentice, the boy had gotten a look and realized how old he was, sixty, sixty-five, face craggy, leathered, slightly sagging, gray and stubbled.

The civilian had heard the first shot as he started from his quarters toward the stables. The time was shortly after 4:00 A.M., and his plan had been to feed his horse, then to get some coffee and bacon at the mess hall, smoke a cigarette, and watch the sun come up. By then the troopers he was on patrol with would be up and ready. He would join them, riding off, checking out the border to the west.

He never reached the stables. Ten feet from the shack that he'd been sleeping in, he heard the first shot and he stopped. He tensed and waited, and the second shot came very fast, and then a countless number all together. He had thought that the rumble was from early morning thunder, but now he understood. Thunder nothing. It was horses, and he had his lever-action rifle as well as his pistol in its holster, reaching for it, pulling back the slide, chambering a round, looking where the shots and horses were, calculating where to head them off.

Over to the right, and he was running past the barracks, seeing muzzle flashes by the warehouse, shacks on fire, hearing riders shouting, horses rumbling, gunshots sounding, running till he had a clear view of the riders, and he fired. Too much going on to tell if he connected. He shot again and ran between two shacks and shot again and then again, using up his magazine, putting in another, shooting at the riders charging past. It was clear that they were Mexican. Aiming at a big-sombreroed horseman with a machete, he swung and fired, dropping the rider, whose foot caught in the stirrup as the horse broke stride and swerved, the horseman, foot still in the stirrup, bouncing, twisting, as he passed.

The civilian kept swinging with the horse and saw the object that the rider had been bearing down on, and he couldn't believe it. Out there in the middle of it all, standing, hands down by his sides and totally defenseless, was a man. No, not even that, a boy, dressed in trooper's pants, no shirt, the top of his underwear showing white against his chest, an easy target, standing motionless, and the horsemen were around him, charging, shooting, and the civilian knew he shouldn't do it, knew it was stupid, but Christ the kid just stood there, and the next thing he himself was bursting from the space between the shacks, rushing toward the kid, crouching, shooting at the riders by him, rushing farther on, and he was so mad that he crashed against the kid, shoulder full against his chest.

They sprawled hard on the ground.

"What is it? Who the—"

"Dammit, you stay down!" And the civilian was so mad at himself that he nearly hit the kid, grabbing at his belt, at the collar of his underwear, dragging, cursing, lunging him. The civilian saw a nearby shack. The door was open, and he threw the kid in, threw the rifle after him, turned, got his bearings, and fired twice at two riders going by.

9

THE rider took it in the neck and toppled. The civilian looked back where the kid was in the shack, saw a muzzle flash from the doorway, knew that he was all right, and forgot about him.

The civilian heard a shot behind him and turning saw a trooper down on one knee by the corner of a building, his rifle steadied, firing. The civilian saw five others, lying flat in a circle, their flanks protected, firing. There were shots from buildings, under wagons, out of ditches, clumps of bushes, horsemen milling, and by now the flames from burning shacks were matched by fires in town that flickered toward the sky.

The civilian saw a string of riders charging toward the fires. He dodged between two buildings, running that way, shooting at a stream of horsemen galloping past the railway station, reached the slope that led up to the tracks, worked up it, paused to make sure there was no one on the other side, and hurried down. The north–south road was filled with milling, shooting riders—that was to his left. To his right were troopers rushing with their carbines toward the town. He ran across an open space, reached a line of houses, dodged a fence, ran down an alley, came out on an east–west street, the flames from burning stores making him squint.

A machine gun crew was in the street, trying to set up. A line of riders turned a corner, charging down on them. A second column joined the first. Later, there would be some question. A captured Mexican would say that their leader never joined the fight, that having given orders he had stayed back in the desert with reserves, what was more that he hadn't used his well-known white horse Siete Leguas, meaning "Seven Leagues," but a roan horse called Taurino. Whatever, the civilian was quite sure that he saw Villa, short and stubby, heavy-chested, almost out of proportion with the huge white horse that he was spurring on. As far back as Villa was, his presence seemed to fill the street, his cold black eyes like smoldering coal.

The machine gun crew was trying desperately to set up. One man hunkered low to fix the tripod while another fed in an ammunition belt, a third one shooting fast to cover them. They never had a chance. The double column of riders just kept coming, shooting, crushing them. The civilian stepped back in the alley and aimed at Villa charging past, flinching as a bullet hit the wall above his head. The civilian aimed again and this time fired, missing, the slide on top of his pistol staying back, showing that his magazine was empty. He reached into his pocket for a fresh one, ejecting the old, saw a shadow come to rest, and looked up at a Mexican on horseback grinning at him. The Mexican was less than ten feet away, and as the horseman grinned, he raised his gun to fire. He never finished. The civilian reached beneath his open vest and drew a second gun, a western-style revolver, lunging toward the horse, coming in beneath its head, forcing it to rear up as he ducked free of the horse's hooves and fired up at the rider. The rider took it in the face. Lurching back, his momentum added to the horse's and forced the horse to keep on rearing, horse and rider tumbling.

▣▣▣▣▣ 10 ▣▣▣▣▣

LATER, a clock stopped by a bullet at the railway station would show that the exact time of the attack was 4:11. There would be some question about Villa's motive for attacking. Two years earlier he had advertised himself as pro-American, welcomed U.S. presidential emissaries,

18

and consulted U.S. military leaders in a well-known meeting on the El Paso–Juárez bridge.

But that had been after four years of civil war in Mexico. The dictator Díaz had been replaced by an apparent popular favorite named Madero. He in turn had been replaced by Huerta. Villa had been fighting for Madero, and with forty thousand troops behind him, had turned against Huerta. It had taken a year, but along with help from the rebel leaders Zapata and Carranza, Villa had won. The problem then was who would rule the country. All along Villa had maintained that he was not a candidate, but when Carranza gained enough support to rule, Villa moved against him. From east to west throughout the north, Carranza–Villa forces clashed.

The U.S. choice was critical. Woodrow Wilson was then president and, with the war in Europe, staunchly isolationist. The Germans, fearing that in time the United States would join the Allies, had sent men and weapons into Mexico. They reasoned that Wilson would never enter overseas if he feared a front in Mexico, and Wilson for his part was determined to see Mexico at peace, the Germans ousted. The issue was which rebel had the strength to unify the country. Carranza had support but so did Villa, and Villa's pro-American attitude made him Wilson's likely choice. But then Villa started losing battles and was rumored to be pro big business, and when Carranza won a labor union endorsement, Wilson, pressed to make a quick decision, chose Carranza. He cut off American arms and food to Villa and at the same time allowed Carranza anything he could.

The conflict came to a head at Agua Prieta, an Arizona–Mexican border town where Villa laid siege to the

Carranza forces barracked there while the United States allowed Carranza's troops to reinforce the town by means of railway shipments through the United States. "The scene was set for a battle that was almost unique in military history," one historian later put it. "Observers were able to watch it from the side lines like a football game. . . . The Villa forces approached, the American trenches were manned, and the American artillery went into previously selected positions shortly before daybreak. . . . Carranzista artillery opened up, and for the rest of the afternoon and the evening there was a heavy exchange of fire between the defenders and the attackers. At one-thirty in the morning Villa launched his assault, his men pushing home their attack . . . all to no avail, for the Villistas learned, as both sides on the Western Front in Europe had already learned, that an assault against a position covered with barbed wire, defended by cross-firing machine guns, supported by artillery firing high explosive, is doomed to failure. For the first time, probably, in Mexican military history, the battlefield was illuminated. Villa's previous success in night attacks caused him to have great faith in them, but at Agua Prieta the night was turned into day by powerful searchlights, the beams of which not only revealed the oncoming attack but blinded the attackers. These searchlights caused much bitterness among the Villistas and quickly added to the grudge that they were building up against the United States. As it became apparent during the next few days that their defeat was helped, if not entirely caused, by the new policies of the United States, rumors began to circulate among the Villistas that the searchlights were furnished by the United States and manned by United States soldiers and, finally, that the lights were located on the United States side of the boundary.''

Bereft of arms, losing battles and morale, Villa's forces gradually deserted him, dwindling from forty thousand to four thousand and then four hundred. Villa took to the desert-mountain country of Chihuahua and, angry at the help the United States gave Carranza, turned his attention against American mining interests in that region, kidnapping managers and holding them for ransom, intercepting fuel and holding that for ransom, storming into camps and looting them. Throughout early 1916, there were various U.S.–Villa clashes of this sort, the most famous of which occurred on January 10 and was called the Santa Isabel massacre when seventeen Americans were taken from a Chihuahua City train and shot as they were going to restart a mine that Villa had shut down. A dog belonging to the Americans was almost sabercut in half, yet somehow lived. A gold ring taken from one body later showed up on a fallen raider at Columbus. From all reports, Villa wasn't at the train. All the same, he ordered what went on there.

Given his strong need for supplies, then, and his sharp change toward America, it isn't surprising that in time Villa should get around to raiding a U.S. border town. Indeed, the United States was expecting it. Reports of Villa's movements near the border came into Fort Bliss at El Paso every day. Garrisons all along the border were ordered to keep watch. Camp Furlong at Columbus was itself responsible for patrolling a sixty-five-mile zone.

But everyone had thought the attack would come at El Paso or at a Mexican town south of Columbus called Palomas. No one understood how badly in need of arms and horses Villa's forces were or how enraged he was at two Columbus storekeepers. Brothers Sam and Louis Ravel ran a hotel and the general store, and when the United States had cut off supplies to Villa, they had refused to give Villa weapons that he had ordered, refusing as well to return the money he had given them. The center of the raid was their hotel and their store, looted first, then burned.

The raid itself was masterful, a sudden night attack that was Villa's trademark. Cutting the international fence several miles west of the border gate, avoiding the outpost there, in the early hours of March 9 he led his men to the outskirts of Columbus and ordered a two-pronged attack, one on the camp, principally the stables and the munitions building, the other on the business heart of town, the store, and the Ravel brothers. The preceding day, Villa had sent two men to town to check the garrison, and they had reported that there were only thirty soldiers. Actually there were three hundred, but during the day most of them had been on patrol, which was why the two men hadn't seen them and why what should have been an easy raid turned into a disaster.

A town of four hundred civilians and three hundred troopers was suddenly added to by another four hundred raiders, all of whom were shooting. The confusion would have been great enough in the daytime, but at night it was much worse, and the list of casualties shows, surprisingly, that only eighteen Americans were killed, eight wounded, against ninety raiders killed, twenty-three wounded, and a lesser number taken prisoner. It is a mark of the American troopers' readiness that they got over their shock as fast as they did and mobilized enough so that what was supposed to have been a lightning-quick raid ended up a three-hour running battle. Even so, Villa got what he wanted. Not counting a considerable amount of food and supplies, his men made off with eighty horses, thirty mules, several wagons full of military equipment, including machine guns, ammunition, and three hundred Mauser rifles. There were no rapes reported.

11

A man rushed with his wife across the east—west street toward the adobe protection of the second hotel. His wife was five months pregnant, her bulging stomach showing clearly as she took a bullet through her fullness. The husband slumped in grief beside her and somehow wasn't killed.

A man, his wife and three-month child beside him, backed their car from their garage to drive away and took a bullet in the shoulder. He reached the north—south road and, hit again, was powerless. His wife climbed into the driver's seat and drove them to the desert.

A family hid within a clump of cactus. Another family hid inside a ditch, guarded by a lieutenant and his brother. When a horseman nearly rode them down, they shot him, only wounding him. Fearful that another shot would draw attention to them, the men ran to the fallen raider, striking at him with a knife. The blade broke off, and while one man held the raider, the other killed him with a gun butt, clubbing him as the lieutenant's wife and daughter huddled in the ditch and looked away, their hands across their ears to muffle the sounds of battered flesh.

Huddled in their bedroom, mattresses against the board walls of their house, a family feared that the crying of their five-month-old baby would attract the raiders to them. The mother stuffed a pillowcase inside the baby's mouth, then looked away. The next time she looked back, the baby wasn't moving. She yanked the gag out, almost screamed, and the baby started breathing.

□□□□□ 12 □□□□□

THE raiders had all passed now. The civilian ran from fallen Mexican to Mexican, checking to make sure they were dead. The light was better, not just from the spreading fires but from the rising sun, and as the civilian looked across the street he saw two Mexicans on foot come from a doorway struggling with a boy who came up to their shoulders and was in his underwear. The two raiders stopped and looked around when they realized that they were all alone. The civilian shot them, firing twice, slamming one down on the wooden sidewalk, the other through a window. Just then the riders turned and galloped back, and the civilian couldn't see the boy.

He ducked back into the alley and, bumping into someone, turned and saw a woman, blood from head to foot, her eyes blank. She had her hands out, trying to reach the street, and grabbing her, the civilian thrust her down beside a barrel. He dropped to one knee, fired at the shooting raiders going past, then ran out beyond the sidewalk and shot at their backs.

The light was even better now, and glancing to make sure there were no more coming, he kept firing as the riders swung around the corner to the left. One rider fell; another doubled over. Then they were gone, and the civilian heard shots from the camp, isolated shots from all around the town. He glanced at the woman in the alley, saw her stumbling, her face bruised, toward the street, saw another woman rushing toward her, pivoted for targets, found none, heard a bugle sound formation, then another sound attack, and grabbing the reins of a fallen rider's horse, careful not to spook it, he swung up into the saddle, the high wide Mexican saddle horn feeling strange to him as he kicked the horse and galloped down the street.

What followed next was one of four remaining mounted pistol charges in U.S. history. The civilian galloped around the corner, down the north–south road, over the railway tracks, past the depot on the left and on the right the customs station, heard volleys of rifle shots to his right, and guessed that they came from troopers firing from the high ground near the flagpole at the retreating raiders. He saw a column of troopers galloping through the camp, saw another column join them from the left, and then both columns angled toward the desert. In the half-dawn sky, the light, however good, was not bright enough to see at any distance, and the dust raised by the charging horses, what the civilian guessed to be near fifty, made sight even worse. He rode to their dust cloud, passed through it, and only then turned right. The cover fire from the camp was dwindling, replaced by shots from the troopers galloping ahead. The troopers turned a little, turned a little more, directly south now, dust cloud rising, galloping, and the civilian nudged the horse to gain on them, coming to one side.

Then in the fast-improving light, with the jerking rise and fall of the horse's hooves on the rocky desert floor, he saw the raiders far ahead, three hundred yards off, maybe more, small bobbing specks in the dust and cactus, riding hard. He passed teams and wagons they'd abandoned, passed bleeding raiders fallen in the dirt. He looked to the right at the strung-out mass of troopers, looked ahead at where the ground sloped down, rode into it, worked on up the other side, and galloped on.

He saw ahead where the raiders had passed a section of high ground, leaving men to shoot and cover them. Bullets kicked up dirt. Two troopers fell, and someone gave the order to pull up. At first the civilian was afraid that they were returning to camp. He reined back his horse, easing to a stop. The others slowly stopped. He looked at them, spread in groups or singly, to his right. They were swallowing, wiping their faces, their shirts dark with sweat, while they held tightly to their reins. The dust cloud settled. Ahead in the now bright distance, the civilian saw glimpses of dust-enshrouded horsemen riding past the high ground, glints off rifles on the hill. The man who'd told them to pull up, Major Tompkins, hatless, dressed in breeches and a work shirt, with a short thin mustache specked with dust, rode among them while they looked at him expectantly, and he looked at the raiders, then at them, and said, "Spread out."

"Yes, *sir*!" a sergeant told him, grinning.

The rest began to grin as well. Because they weren't going back to camp at all. This was the start of the sequence of orders for attack formation, and given the disheveled pattern they had stopped in, the civilian had to marvel at how quickly they got into line, each man in his squad, each squad in its place, abreast of each other, facing toward the defended hill. He nudged his horse, moving into place on the left end of the line, watching as the major, riding up and down to make sure they were braced, came down and stopped and looked at him. The civilian nodded. The major nodded back. Then, looking at his men, the major told them, "Check your pistols," but they were well ahead of him, sliding out the old magazines, exchanging them for new, checking the smooth top actions on their handguns, slipping in the new magazines in a long uneven string of metallic clicks as the magazines slid home. They sat tense and ready, clenching their pistols so hard that the whites of their knuckles showed.

The major looked at them once more and told them, "On the walk."

"Yes, *sir*," the sergeant told him and repeated, and they started, a single straight line, abreast of each other, almost as if this were a race and it was important that they all begin together.

They moved slowly forward for a short time, letting the horses get their breath, feeling the rhythm of the advance together. Then the major told them, "On the trot," and the sergeant echoed, and then it was "Canter," and the whole sequence was like a great machine starting up, smooth and large and powerful, almost impossible to stop, dust rising behind the civilian, the troopers to the right of him holding their reins left-handed, their right hands ready with their pistols.

Then it was "Gallop," and this time the sergeant didn't need to repeat the order. The horses were caught up in the rhythm, straining to get on with this, and all the troopers needed to do was loosen control, and the horses were charging at a gallop, the hill that the rear guard of the raiders was defending looming up on them, flashes from rifles, bullets flying toward them, as one by one the troopers stood high in their stirrups, leaning forward, and the major told them, "Fire!"

Leaning forward, pistols aimed above their horses' heads, just between the ears, they started, bullets sounding, recoils jerking, empty magazines ejecting, and it was like a wagon full of magazines dumped into a fire, report after report rolling off across the flat empty desert plain, fifty pistols, seven rounds to a magazine, and the line was almost to the hill now, bullets ricocheting off rocks, cacti splintering, the Mexicans up there firing, and the middle line held back a little as the flanks moved forward and the troopers started up the contour of the hill, the column in a semicircle, firing, charging, some out of bullets now, ejecting empty magazines, slamming in new ones, standing, firing. All the rocks and cacti at the top were virtually exploding, raiders dropping, falling back, the troopers charging, and then they reached the top and there was no one, bodies all around but horsemen already down the other side. Some troopers started after them, the major shouting, "Halt!" while the others slipped down off their horses, grabbing at their rifle scabbards. The major shouted, "Halt!" again. The sergeant echoed him. They had to shout it yet again before the troopers riding down there listened, reining hard and turning while the men who'd grabbed their rifles started firing. They were on their chests or kneeling, strung out on the summit, shooting, horsemen down there dropping, and then the troopers who had started down were up on top again, and they were off their horses, grabbing for their rifles, firing, still more horsemen dropping, then less, then merely specks of rising dust down there for targets, and the major said, "Cease fire." A few of them kept on. "Cease fire!" the sergeant told them. And they stopped.

A wind came up, blowing bits of sand against them. No one moved. Then someone coughed. Another, on his stomach, rifle poised, rolled over on his back. Another wiped his mouth. "Christ," another said, and it was over.

They glanced at one another, felt themselves to see if they were hurt. They checked their horses flecked with lather. The major looked around and glanced at the civilian.

"How long till they lead us to the border?"

The civilian didn't understand. Then he realized. The major must have been so caught up in the chase that he hadn't even registered the wide strip of cutaway fence they had passed through. The civilian pushed back his hat and wiped his sweaty forehead. Then he pointed.

"Major, I'd say we passed it four miles back."

The major didn't move. He just kept looking at him. Then he glanced at the ground and shook his head, and when he looked up, his eyes were clear and he was grinning. Not much, not so that his teeth were showing, but enough, and the civilian grinned as well and nodded.

"Sergeant," the major said. "Send a courier back to camp. Have him tell the colonel what we've done and ask him for instructions."

"Yes, sir."

"Wait a moment. Let's be more specific. Have him find out from the colonel if we may continue."

"Yes, *sir*," the sergeant said.

They waited forty minutes. When the man came back, it turned out that the colonel had avoided taking responsibility by telling the major to use his judgment. "My judgment's to continue."

So they mounted up and started off, and apparently the Mexicans hadn't thought the troopers would pursue, because one hour later the troopers caught up to them again and there was another running battle and then another and they kept on like that all morning until finally the Mexicans stopped leaving rear guards to protect themselves and turned their full three hundred men against the pursuing fifty troopers, and the Americans had no choice but to stand ground and reorganize.

Each group formed a line that stared across four hundred yards. By that time it was noon, no food or water, horses winded, ammunition low, and after an hour's wait for the Mexicans to attack, the major ordered a withdrawal. The return was slow, horses drooping, the sun at its hottest, men almost slipping from their saddles, but along the way they counted thirty Mexican bodies and picked up several wagons full of food and clothing, two machine guns, and a dozen cases of guns and ammunition. All along the dusty route, riderless horses wandered. The civilian helped to round them up.

▯▯▯▯▯ 13 ▯▯▯▯▯

PRENTICE grabbed the boots around the ankles. The man on detail with him grabbed the wrists. They lifted, dragging, backs bent, scraping, toward the fire. Even with the handkerchief around his nose and mouth, tied behind his neck, he couldn't keep from gagging. He nodded to the man beside him, and they lifted higher, swinging the body back and forth until on the count of three they heaved and let it go. It arced through the air, sank through the flames, and flopped down on the topmost body of the pile. The flames spread through the corpse's hair, orange and white, black smoke swirling. Prentice had to turn away, the sound of broiling meat, fat bubbling, dripping behind him. He walked back to the row of bodies, stacked like cords of wood, and looked down at the insects on them, little hardcased bugs all over, running in and out of their clothes and wounds and open mouths.

And the flies. Prentice had heard that in the desert there weren't any flies, but it was obvious he'd heard wrong. Because the flies had settled now as well, and in the midday heat the corpses had already started puffing up, and even wearing gloves, even just touching the boots, feeling the flesh beneath, Prentice was sickened.

He looked to his right, toward town. The buildings were low and square, two hundred yards away. It was more than an hour since the last wagon full of corpses had come down, and they had all been picked up near the outskirts, so he guessed that there would be few more. Even so, there were enough. Forty bodies burned so far, another fifty in the pile, and it looked as though they were going to have to start another fire. Something spattered loudly behind him, and he didn't turn. Over there in town they would be cleaning up, a couple days' work at least, one whole block burned out, another close to half, charred wood, twisted metal, broken glass and pots and God knows what all, carting it away from town, replacing boards and windows, mending fences. There had been some surprises and disgraces. The kitchen detail, already up and preparing breakfast, had been in their adobe kitchen when the attack occurred, and, burst in on by raiders, they had defended themselves with anything they had at hand, throwing boiling water on them, hitting one with an ax, another with a baseball bat, finally getting at the shotguns that they used for hunting game and blasting the raiders back through the door. In contrast, the sanitary detachment—another name for medics—had locked themselves in the hospital and refused to go out or let others in. The munitions building had been locked, and members of the machine gun troop had been forced to break the door down. Even then, the machine guns hadn't been much good. Made in France by Benét-Mercié, they almost never worked. Sand kept getting into them, and while they had few moving parts, the actions needed frequent cleaning. More important, they were very hard to load. Their thirty-bullet magazine had to be flipped sideways, wide side facing up, and then inserted into a narrow slot on the right side of the gun. A frustrating job in daylight, it had been intolerable at night.

The first gun had jammed outright. The remaining three had been a long time getting ready. Nonetheless, Prentice had heard a machine gun trooper say that they'd fired twenty thousand rounds.

And he believed it. The stores in town were now a splintered shambles, as were the barracks and the stables. From all reports, there wasn't a building in town that hadn't been hit. If one machine gun crew had shot that much, how many shots on both sides had there been all told? A hundred thousand? Maybe half again as much? He couldn't know. There was a crew in town whose only job was collecting empty bullet casings.

He looked back at the burning bodies, bright orange flames among the black smoke swirling skyward, grabbed another pair of boots, his partner at the wrists, and lifted, dragging. There had been some talk in town of stripping the bodies, taking the boots, but in the end no one had wanted the clothes anyhow and all they'd taken were their weapons, money, and ammunition magazines. That had all been done in town, and Prentice was grateful. Occasionally he would see a knife or a holstered handgun, less often some kind of purse, and throw it over by the road. Mostly he just lifted bodies, dragged and heaved them, fighting not to think. Something caught his eye, and, looking southward past the fire, he saw a double column riding from the desert toward the road. The troopers who had chased the raiders. They must have used the smoke from the burning bodies as a guide.

Closer now, gone more than seven hours and looking it, dust from head to foot, faces parched, horses white with sweat, and they were picking up the smell of the bodies now, pulling out bandannas, covering their noses and their mouths. Some started coughing. They reached the road and turned up past the fire toward town, staring at him and his partner as they passed. A few were cursing.

There was an officer, a major, at their lead, and the sergeant Prentice had talked with at the station. But the one he noticed most was the civilian. Not just because he was the only civilian in the troop but because, even though he himself had only seen the civilian for a few seconds, there was no mistaking his big chest and shoulders and broad face. It was the man who had knocked him down in the night, the man whose rifle he had used. The man looked even older now, his face streaked with sweat and dust, the wrinkles in his face showing clearly like the cracks in sun-parched wood. He was the biggest, most commanding man Prentice had ever seen, and as the civilian passed on this side of the column, the man looked down at him, not long, not hard, more like a glance yet something more than that, then at the pile of burning bodies, then ahead.

Prentice couldn't tell if he had been recognized.

The other troopers kept coming, staring at the fire and the bodies, hands over their faces, gagging, looking away.

"Who is that?" Prentice asked the man on duty with him.

"Major Tompkins."

"No. I mean the civilian with the sergeant."

"The civilian? What civilian?" The man looked at the column for a moment, frowned, and shook his head, and told him, "I don't know."

□□□□□ 14 □□□□□

THE sergeant moved along the food line, poured himself a cup of coffee, turned, and told him, "Calendar."

Prentice didn't understand.

"That's his name. Miles Calendar. What do you want to know for?"

The mess hall was half full, soldiers eating at the rough-planked tables, others coming in to wait in line.

"I have to give him something. Do you know where I can find him?"

"Over in the livery shed, but I wouldn't bother him if I was you."

Prentice waited while the sergeant got a plate of beans and beef, then told him "Thanks," and turned.

"Hey, did you hear what I just said?"

But Prentice was already going out the door.

□□□□□ 15 □□□□□

HE knocked, and no one answered. He opened the door, and in the strip of sunlight that came in behind him, he saw the old man stretched out on the dirt floor, his neck against a sack of grain. His hat was across his face, his arms across his chest, motionless, asleep.

Prentice didn't know if he should move to wake him.

"What is it, boy?" The old man's voice came muffled from beneath his hat.

Prentice tried but couldn't speak.

"Come on, boy. Get it out. You can see I'm trying to sleep."

"I came to thank you."

"All right, you thanked me."

"I mean for when you knocked me down last night."

"I know that's what you mean. No need to rub it in. I was a damn fool taking the chance to bother with you. I could have been dead. It was a mistake."

This wasn't what Prentice had expected. He'd felt good coming to thank the man, and now he was angry. "Well, I'm grateful anyhow. And for the rifle. I've brought it back."

"Did you clean it?"

"Yes," and now he was even more angry.

"Then put it by that crate." The civilian motioned with his boot.

Prentice hesitated, then did what he was told, and waited, neither of them speaking.

"Was there something else?"

"I guess not."

"Then close the door as you go out."

Prentice felt his face go red. Stepping out, he swung the door shut, not exactly in a slam but loud enough that it might as well have been.

▣▣▣▣▣ 16 ▣▣▣▣▣

THE old man uncrossed his arms from where he'd had one hand on the gun beneath his vest, pulled up his hat, and looked at the rifle by the door. He glanced at the door, heard the boy walk off, boots crunching in the dirt, and wiped his hand across his face.

▣▣▣▣▣ 17 ▣▣▣▣▣

WHAT happened next was largely in reaction to what had happened to Maud Wright. She was one of several Americans then living in Mexico, in her case 120 miles south of the border on a small ranch near a town called Pearson in Chihuahua. On March 1, eight days before the raid on Columbus, she and her baby daughter had been waiting alone on the ranch for her husband and a friend of his to come back from buying supplies in Pearson, when twelve armed horsemen rode through the gate and dismounted at the house. These were a scouting party from Villa's main force, which was on its way north toward the border.

At first they pretended to be soldiers for Villa's enemy, President Carranza, and they asked her if she had some food to sell. She told them all she had was a little flour and some cornmeal, just enough for the family, and when they asked again if they could buy it, she said she would give it to them.

By then it was dark. Maud's husband and his friend came back from Pearson with two loaded pack mules, which the raiders took. The raiders tied her husband and his friend, stripped the house of everything they could, took her baby, gave it to a local peasant, put Maud on a mule, and told her she was going with them. She couldn't see her husband. She called. He didn't answer. She scrambled off the mule, rushing toward her baby. A soldier drew his sword and said that he would kill her. He forced her onto the mule again, and, as she later said, she knew that she was trapped.

The march north lasted from the first until the ninth. The scouting party joined the rest of Villa's force, and they never rested more than three hours out of twenty-four. Maud went to Villa, begging him to let her go. He told her to complain to his subordinates—that's what they were for. She went to his subordinates. They told her to shut up, that they intended her to ride until she dropped. Nine days through the desert of Chihuahua, little food, less water, eyes glazed, slumped in her saddle, buzzards circling overhead. Villa told her that the life she led with him was good for her: "Your cheeks are rosy and fat." "Sunburnt and swollen," she said. And when they finally reached Columbus, he told her he was going to make her shoot some people in the town. She told him she would shoot him first, and he just laughed.

But when the raid went badly, the men who guarded Maud released her, and she stumbled through the desert toward the town. She came across a woman who'd been wounded and helped to get her to a doctor. She helped with wounded in the camp. Then people realized what she had been through, and they made her get some rest. She slept one whole day and night, had the first full meal she'd eaten in nine days, found out that her husband had been killed but that her baby was alive, and said that she was going to walk back to Pearson.

"I want my baby. It'll only take nine days."

Her story appeared on the front page of every major newspaper in the United States. There were several follow-ups, and even though it turned out that she never did walk back to Pearson, that she was taken to El Paso, where her baby was delivered to her, the details she recalled made constant vivid copy: how Villa had planned to make torches out of every man, woman, and child in Columbus, how he intended to kill every American he could and would be helped by Japan and Germany, how early in the march he'd come across an American on the road. A score of his men had trampled the man. One officer had dragged him past a company. Another had shot him in the neck, and the man had run close to forty feet before he dropped. They'd stripped him of his clothing and divided it. The column had ridden their horses over him, and the last man shot him in the head.

Details like those, coupled with Maud's experience, made Columbus real. It was one thing to talk about eighteen Americans killed, eight others wounded, but that was abstract. Even reports of atrocities in Columbus tended to emphasize only the facts. What was needed was a full, fleshed-out story that appealed to American sentiment, and Maud Wright's ordeal provided that. A woman whose home had been ransacked, whose husband had been killed, whose baby had been taken from her—these elements seemed peculiarly designed to stir up American wrath. All that was missing were a flag and an apple pie, and considering that America's boundaries had been violated, the flag was involved nonetheless. By the morning of the tenth, Congress was in debate. By the eleventh, it had decided to send an expedition into Mexico.

The ostensible purpose was to cut off Villa's movement southward, lest he next attack a settlement of American Mormons 160 miles below the border at a place called Colonia Dublán. The real purpose was to have an excuse to cross the border, catch Villa's forces, and annihilate them. There was some confusion on this point. At first the order was simply to catch Villa, but, as the Army Chief of Staff explained, that was in effect to make war on one man, and if Villa got on a train to go to Guatemala, Yucatán, or even South America, the United States couldn't very well go after him. What was really needed was to render him inoperative, and that meant going after his men more than Villa himself.

The plan involved five thousand troops, a full one-sixth of the then existing state-based U.S. forces. As a further measure, one senator proposed a bill to authorize recruiting more than half a million troops, and while most thought that seemed too great an escalation, the military considered it inadequate.

"We have now been occupying the Mexican frontier for more than four years," one colonel told an audience in

New York, his speech reprinted in *The New York Times*. "At the present moment two-thirds of our regular army that is in the United States is on that border. In other words, we have twenty-two thousand soldiers scattered along the frontier.

"You do not realize the extent of that frontier. It takes a full three days by train to go from one end to the other, and along that line you have twenty-two thousand men, and the number available to reinforce them in the event it becomes necessary is just about nine thousand. If it was not so pathetic, it would be farcical.

"Until this war in Europe broke, the U.S. Army looked to you like the fly seen through the magnifying end of a telescope. I tell you that the American Army is the most pathetic thing that ever came along, and other nations know this even better than ourselves. . . . The time has come when you must realize that when in 1898 we departed from the policy of a century and announced ourselves a world power we assumed certain obligations, and you must realize that in order to carry out those obligations it is necessary that we have force behind every note that our president may find it necessary to send, or any other act that a president may find necessary in the proper performance of his duties.

"What do you think it would mean if we went to war with England, Germany, France, or some other first-class power? Americans, you know, have a way of going about with a chip on their shoulders every time something happens to their trade. We are pretty well informed that England now has four million men ready to take their place in the battle line, that Germany has from six million to eight million, and Russia from eight million to ten million. Commercially we are also now in competition with a nation to the west.

"I believe it is worthy of serious thought to keep in mind that if we are involved on the Atlantic we will be struck at the same time on the Pacific. Four million men could come from the Atlantic and three million more from the Pacific, and four million plus three million makes seven million. How are you going to meet such a situation if it arises? We have a coast line of at least twenty thousand miles, vulnerable at every point except where we have some harbor defenses, and these defenses are manned by only one relief.

"We can raise a regular army of one hundred and forty thousand men, perhaps one of two hundred thousand, but when you get beyond those figures the price becomes prohibitive for we have to go out into the open market and compete for men, because like a bunch of idiots we have been living under what we call a volunteer system of enlistments.

"There is only one course that common sense dictates, and that is to train the youth of our land and to begin that training when they are young. You have got to train these boys. You have got to force them to train if necessary."

The first American Aero Squadron was formed, the first American Auto-Truck Companies shortly after; state militias mobilized. And all through preparations, the United States tried to get consent from Mexico to enter. Years before, there had been an agreement between the two countries that allowed each other's forces to cross the border in pursuit of hostile Indians. Now Carranza's government proposed that agreement once again. Mexico would be allowed to pursue outlaws into the United States, and the United States in turn could go after bandits into Mexico *"if the raid effected at Columbus should unfortunately be repeated."* On the face of it, the United States had permission, but only in the future. Clearly, Carranza did not want American troops in Mexico at the present time, but America was enraged and in a hurry, and the qualifier was ignored.

And so Columbus grew. The three-times-daily train that Prentice had come in on now came ten and twenty times a day, dropping off men and horses and supplies; field cannons, cases of ammunition, rifles, and machine guns. An airstrip was begun on the bottom edge of camp near the north–south road. A ramp was begun, two strips of concrete with a space between: the first U.S. Army motor pool. Twenty trucks, then fifty, then a hundred; fifteen motorcycles and assorted cars. A thousand troops, then another, and another. The camp doubled, then doubled again. The town grew in proportion.

🆒🆒🆒🆒🆒 **18** 🆒🆒🆒🆒🆒

"GENTLEMEN, we're going, unofficially you understand, to invade Mexico."

The soldiers looked as if they hadn't heard, not that they hadn't been listening but that the words simply hadn't registered. The sergeant waited while they put down pitchforks, curry combs, and saddle polish, staring at him. Then he continued.

"That's right—Mexico. You can figure on leaving by sun-up the day after tomorrow, so if any of you have got letters to write or boots to mend or buttons to sew, you'd best get at them. And while you're at it, say your prayers because, believe me, once you get down there, God help you. . . . God help us all.

"In case any of you signed up, figuring to pass the time up in some green-grass country to the east, waiting for us to jump into that German thing overseas, you might as well know what we're getting into. You'll be riding south through ninety-four thousand square miles of the God damnedest, most barren and sun-bleached pile of rocks and dust that the good Lord ever took an unholy inclination to think up, called Chihuahua province."

In the back stall, leaning on the shoulder-high partition, his face streaked with sweat and flecked with dust from cleaning out the dirty straw and putting in new, Prentice looked beyond the men ahead of him toward the sergeant talking to them, and then at the men themselves—if that's what they could be called—the youngest, newest troops in camp. And it bothered him that he had been put on detail with them. Not that he wasn't young and new himself—he had certainly demonstrated that—and not that this kind of job wasn't what he and they deserved. But he recalled the way that he had acted during the attack, and he thought that they might act the way he had; what was more, that he himself might act the same way again. The way to handle this, it seemed to him, was to mix them in with seasoned troops and let them get the feel of things. Cut off this way, they'd have no one to imitate.

The stable had no walls on this side, just a roof and poles supporting it. He looked from the men and the sergeant talking to them past the other stalls and the bales of straw toward the open air and the preparations going on in camp. There had been some talk about their going into Mexico, but most had thought that they were going to reinforce the border. Now they knew better. Mule-drawn wagons hauling crates. Troopers herding horses. Others roping off corrals. And just for a second, out there in the sun and dust, his head high above two soldier-wranglers, pointing toward a group of horses, was Calendar.

Then another string of horses passed between, and Calendar was gone, and the sergeant kept on talking.

"You'll be riding nonstop for as long as you can take it, eating, sleeping, cursing in your saddles, so sick of your horses by the time you're through you'll swear that they're the very likeness of the devil. You'll pray for rain, but there won't be any. You'll dream of food, but all you'll get is beans and bread. And all the time you're down there after Villa, the Mexican federals will be after *you* because some damn fools in Mexico got to arguing with us, and now we're going in without their blessing."

"Sergeant, how long will it take?"

The sergeant looked hard at the skinny kid who'd interrupted, uncertain how to treat the question, then decided. "The major told me the colonel told him six weeks, but if you ask me it'll be more like six months or even a year. That's why I'm going on like this. You'll hear a lot of talk about how we're going down there and cleaning this up and coming back before anybody knows it, but don't you believe a word. It's the same kind of talk that says let's ship out and show them Frenchmen how to fight them

45

Germans, and it's all dead wrong. The raiders' trail is a couple days old by now. We'll have a hell of a time following it. Most places the ground is too hard, and other places sandstorms fill the prints in, and we can't depend on villagers showing us the way—Villa's been either feeding them or scaring them too long. So you figure on the worst, and if something better comes along, no harm done. But don't count on it. . . . That's the only way I know to prepare you.''

Prentice looked at the sergeant, then past the stalls and the bales of straw toward the open once again, and the string of horses had gone past, showing as their dust cloud settled the civilian, his back turned, no mistaking him however, big and solid even at this distance, walking toward a group of soldiers, nodding toward a row of barrels, pointing where to move them.

□□□□□ 19 □□□□□

"DID you give him what you wanted?''

Prentice heard the sergeant's voice behind him. It was later, and he was still on duty. Not because he hadn't finished—the others were gone now—but because he wanted to keep busy and this was what he knew and besides Calendar was still at work out there and he wanted to keep watching him. He brushed the horse's flank once more, looked over to where Calendar was straining to rig up a picket line, put down the brush, and turned. "Oh yeah, I gave it to him all right. For all the good it did me."

The sergeant shrugged. "I warned you fair enough. He's a strange one. Does his job, keeps to himself, won't let anybody close to him." The sergeant thought about it. "I never met a man yet who claimed him as a friend, excepting maybe the major, and even then I don't guess the major thinks of it exactly as a friendship. They just work together well from when they were in the Philippines."

"The Philippines?" Humid air and rain and jungle seemed to Prentice so out of place that he repeated it.

"Oh, sure. The way I hear it, he's been in 'em all, right back to the Civil War."

"What?" Prentice couldn't quite believe it. "How old must he be anyhow?"

"Close to sixty-five." The sergeant shrugged again. "I figured it out once. He must have been thirteen or fourteen back then. After that he was a trooper and then a scout in the Indian Wars. Then he signed on again in Cuba, and the Philippines like I said, and now here. There's not a man on this post knows more about this business than he does. We get in trouble down there and you see there's more than an even chance you'll be killed, you stick close to him. Do what he does. No question, it'll be the right thing."

They stood there looking out at Calendar. "Kind of sad in a way," the sergeant said.

"How's that?"

"Well, sixty-five, this'll be his last. The Army won't hire him anymore, not with that German thing brewing. Doesn't matter how good he still is, they won't take a

47

chance on him starting to make mistakes. He's a career man who's strung it out as far as he can, and it won't be long before he'll have no place to go. That's what I mean by sad. Ten years from now I'll be in his place myself.''

Prentice looked at the sergeant, then back out there, and the sun was almost down, tinting Calendar that peculiar reddish brown as he stood up on a wagon, dumping water barrels so they spilled down over the corral fence into a trough.

🁢🁢🁢🁢🁢 20 🁢🁢🁢🁢🁢

THE old man watched the horses with their heads down drinking. The one kept nudging another until the other had enough and nipped at her and that was that. The old man had to laugh.

He turned and saw the major coming toward him, eased down over the side, and touched the ground. Even so, his left leg almost buckled, and he had to brace himself to stand. The major didn't look as if he'd noticed. ''Exactly how bad is it, Miles?''

At first the old man thought he meant his leg, and then he understood. He breathed and shook his head. ''As bad as I'd care to think. These horses all have shipping fever. They just keep passing blood. They need at least two weeks fattening on the best grain we can buy which we don't have or enough wagons to haul it if we did have or enough wagons to haul water. Once we get down there all we've got is alkaline water and Chihuahua grass that a horse can eat all year and still not gain a pound on, we don't need to worry about meat for the men, you're looking at it.''

"Sure, Miles," the major said and grinned at him. "But will we get down and back from there all right?"

"They've told us to, haven't they? Of course we will."

Then they both were grinning, and the major pulled out two cigars.

21

OVER in the stable, Prentice watched them, haloed by the setting sun, the major lighting Calendar's cigar and then his own, the two men walking toward the mess hall, talking, chuckling, blowing smoke from their cigars. He kept on watching until they reached the mess hall and passed by it, out of sight.

□□□□□ **22** □□□□□

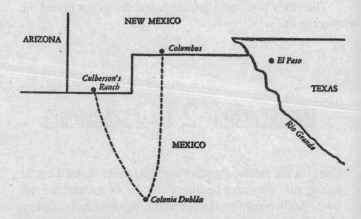

THE plan called for three columns heading into Mexico, one from El Paso to the east, the second from Columbus in the middle, the third from a ranch, owned by a man named Culberson, near the Arizona border to the west. The idea was to form a kind of triangle, forcing the raiders to the center where the Columbus column, working down that way, could pick them off.

But the sweep down from El Paso was dependent on the use of Mexican railways, and the Mexican government refused permission, so the eastern sweep was canceled, and the two remaining columns went down separately, not so much because of tactics as logistics. Both forces were considerable, and rather than first combine them, it seemed easier to set them on their own and let them come together later on.

The sergeant had been wrong. They didn't leave at daybreak as he'd said. The camp was so large that the column didn't get organized until almost noon. Prentice waited while they cranked up trucks and finished loading wagons, standing with his company on the road beside the camp, holding tight-reined to his horse. It was no better and no worse than other standard mounts, only different. A gelded cross between Arabian and quarter, it combined the best of both, speed coupled with endurance, chestnut brown with a white strip down its face, small enough that Prentice didn't have to stretch to mount, big enough to carry him and his thirty pounds of gear, eight years old he guessed from its teeth and the way they were slightly worn. He'd been assigned it only yesterday and he'd had a chance to ride it only twice, but the horse felt good beneath him and responded to commands, and if it skittered from the motors and it needed extra girth, so did the others. While the right eye seemed a little better than the left, in time he'd know enough to compensate. Indeed, from his constant grooming and attention, he would know each part of it as well as any horse he'd ever owned.

It shivered as he touched it now, while other motors started up. Troopers rode by down the road, raising dust that settled on him and the horse. Prentice looked at all the men in front and back of him, seasoned soldiers as he'd hoped, the new men he'd been working with dispersed throughout the troop. He looked at other horsemen riding by, saw companies across from him mount up. Then the sergeant came and ordered them to mount as well, and as he did, boot in the stirrup, left hand on the horse's mane, right hand with the reins upon the saddle's pommel, swinging up, he saw the column forming down the road, riders four abreast, regimental colors at the front. Each company was riding by in order, going down to stop and wait in line. Soon his would go as well. In time the wagons and the trucks, the pack mules, and more riders.

He waited, squinting through the rising dust for Calendar, saw instead the major and the colonel. They were coming from a building, talking, then saluting. The major walked across an open stretch to greet a woman and a small boy and a girl. There were other groups like that nearby, officers approaching, and the major stooped to kiss his little girl, handing her a tiny brightly wrapped present, looking at his boy, handing him a present, lifting him, then turning to his wife and kissing her, not long, not hard, on the lips but it might as well have been on the cheek. Prentice saw the major talking to her. Then he heard the sergeant say, "Move out," and, startled, looking at the sergeant, then at the major, he eased off on the reins, squeezed his knees against the horse's girth, and started.

That's when he saw Calendar. In the middle of an open space, troopers riding near, dust around him, sitting motionless on horseback, staring toward the major, Calendar was watching as the major kissed his wife again. Then the major stepped back, turned, and started toward him, and a line of troopers intervened, and Prentice couldn't see him anymore. Riding forward, he strained to look back, but couldn't see.

In a while he stopped as the troopers stopped ahead of

him. Others stopped behind him. Then he heard the motors sounding louder as the trucks moved into line back there. Soon the major rode past up the line, Calendar behind. Someone said, "Move out," again. Prentice made out troopers' hats in motion up there. Calendar came riding back. Prentice turned to watch him go. The next time he looked forward, the horse ahead of him was moving, and he followed.

They crossed the border a little before one o'clock. It was March 15, six days since the raid. There was some fear that the border would be blocked to them, but there weren't any soldiers waiting for them, just a man, a small boy, and a dog, and in an hour the column was in a rhythm, riding down a sun-baked road that soon became a trail and then an indistinguishable part of rock and sand and cactus. In the heat and dust and movement of the column, some troopers out of boredom started singing, sporadically at first, then in a pattern, others joining in. The sergeant laughed, and when someone asked him why, he said the tune that they were singing. "Maybe they don't know it, but it's Villa's marching song."

> *La cucaraaacha*
> *La cucaraaacha*

The second column left the ranch to the west twelve hours later, a little after midnight. The border there was undefended too, and while the Columbus column had set out in midday heat, the air so dry the troopers didn't seem to sweat yet needed water all the time, the western column went through nighttime cold so bad it froze the water in canteens. At first the ground was flat and easy. Then it turned to ruts and breaks, dust from nine months without rain, ankle deep and kicked up white and bitter so it powdered them. It burned their eyes; it clogged the noses of their horses, drying them. They tied bandannas to their faces. They had to stop and tie rags to their horses' muzzles. The mule train fell behind. The horsemen froze. The footmen, closer to the swirling dust, worked harder than the rest and felt the cold less, shifting nine-pound rifles, hunching shoulders underneath their heavy packs. Some, who knew the desert well, had equipped themselves with driver's goggles, but the dust kept filming them, and the more they wiped the dust away, the more the goggles streaked and blurred.

They stopped at dawn, set off again at noon, and where before they'd wished for heat, now they wished for cold. Thirty miles, fifty, sixty. A nighttime stop, then off again, and twelve hours later they were at the rendezvous.

The man who pushed them that hard was named Pershing. A brigadier general, nicknamed Black Jack for the two years he had once spent as a white man with a Negro regiment in Montana, he had been in charge of Fort Bliss at El Paso when the raid occurred. A few years earlier he had talked with Villa there, had even had his picture taken with him. Now, at fifty-five, Pershing was after him. The problem for the War Department had been whom to choose. They needed someone who'd seen action: Pershing had been under fire in Cuba and the Philippines. They needed someone who had knowledge of guerrilla warfare: Cuba and the Philippines again. More than that, they needed someone who could lead an expedition into Mexico and yet not cause a war. Pershing's experience there was crucial. First, as commander of Fort Bliss, he knew the problems of the border. Second, his trademark was to understand his enemy before he went against him. Thus, in all his contests, particularly in the Philippines, he had learned the local language, customs, and religion, approaching the other side on its terms rather than his own. The technique worked so well that many tribes surrendered once they saw good faith. Those who didn't, and this too was a trademark, he annihilated. A peculiar blend of strength and consideration, of readiness to fight yet willingness to listen, Pershing seemed to have the perfect talents for the Mexican campaign. Plus, he didn't seem political. While his wife was the daughter of a senator, Pershing had not used influence as a help in his promotions. Even as it was, his promotions had come readily enough. He had by-passed eight hundred senior officers to make general, and when some had cried connections, Teddy Roosevelt himself had noted that the promotion had come from distinguished service in the Philippines. Pershing's inclination to gain power without seeking it was another factor that made him a good choice for the Mexican campaign. A certain kind of leader might go down there, it was feared, and try to draw attention to himself, blundering into trouble with the Mexican authorities at the expense of U.S. foreign policy. Pershing, on the other hand, could be counted on to do the job yet be invisible. In this judgment, anyhow, his superiors were a slight bit wrong. While not political, Pershing nonetheless was prudent. He took advantage of the Mexican campaign to train his troops for a pitched war overseas, just in case, so that when America entered World War I, as anyone could see that it was going to, the United States had a core of trained troops ready for the fight, and Pershing found himself commander of what was called America's Expeditionary Forces against Germany. But that was all to come.

🀰🀰🀰🀰🀰 23 🀰🀰🀰🀰🀰

THERE was a body in the road before them, dead about a week, the surgeon guessed. The corpse might have been American. After the sun and the coyotes, it was hard to tell. The man had been blindfolded, shot in the head, stripped of shoes and pants and wallet. The column stopped and buried him. The chaplain said some prayers, and they moved on.

Up ahead, the major sent for Calendar. "The map says there are some towns up front. Take the Indians. Check them out."

Calendar refused.

"Why?"

Calendar shook his head. "The Indians. I'm not about to work with them."

"God dammit, Miles."

"I don't care. They weren't in the bargain."

"Well, take the white scouts then. I don't care. Take whoever the hell you want. Just so you check those towns."

Calendar nodded, turning.

Prentice watched him go.

Then above the muffled dusty plodding of the horses

and the rattled chugging of the trucks behind him, Prentice heard a different sound, a high-pitched driving roar that was a different kind of motor. It was faint at first, then growing stronger all the while, and it seemed to come from behind him. The column had just gone down a slope, leveling at the bottom, and turning back the way he'd come, Prentice saw the tail end of the column, then the peak of the hill and other troopers staring back as he was. The noise was even louder. The peak was cloaked with dust, distorted by the heat, the front of a truck just barely showing at the top of the hill. The truck got bigger, wider. The noise got deeper, louder, as the truck detached itself, the heat waves playing tricks of sight, except that the truck was no truck but a plane and it was flying now. It had been all along, a biwinged, linen-covered Curtiss "Jenny," that's what Prentice had heard them called in camp, so frail and shaking that the wonder was that it had ever left the ground. It flew directly along the column, low enough to spook the horses. Even so, some troopers raised their arms and, cheering, waved. The pilot dipped his wings and, motor roaring, waved as well, his leather helmet and goggles showing clearly. Then as fast as he had come up on them he was past, figure shrinking, motor dimming, becoming a speck. The other plane came over less than thirty seconds later.

🔲🔲🔲🔲🔲 24 🔲🔲🔲🔲🔲

IT crashed about a mile ahead.

Calendar was stretched out on a bluff, his field glasses shielded, staring down toward what the map said was a village but was only four adobe shacks. He saw two chickens and a burro but no people, certainly no federals, and crawling back to stand, he heard the plane, over to his left, not one but two he saw now, the lead one flying easily, the second losing height. At first he thought that it was going down deliberately. But then he heard its engine miss, and miss again, and stop. It angled down behind a peak of rocks. Calendar was on his horse before he heard the crash.

🔲🔲🔲🔲🔲 25 🔲🔲🔲🔲🔲

HE met with the other scouts and went down to the wreckage.

"What the hell is this?"

The plane was in a gully, one wheel on a rock, the other in some cactus, wings sheared off, the fuselage somehow

58

intact although snapped and cracked in what appeared a hundred places.

"Pershing's secret weapon," the pilot told them. He was limping from the wreck, cursing, so distracted by his rage that he didn't even seem surprised to see them. "We're supposed to be flying messages, but really if you ask me all we have to do is pass over Villa, lose control, and scare him to death by making him think we're going to crash on him. Christ, look at this thing. No parts, no fuel. Would you believe I've got half an old Ford engine in this crate?" The pilot kicked the side of the fuselage, and the whole thing fell apart.

▣▣▣▣▣ 26 ▣▣▣▣▣

THE pilot of the first plane didn't know his partner had gone down until five minutes after he passed the column, looked back, and saw the empty sky. Even so, he went a little farther, thinking maybe he'd misjudged the distance, that the plane was back there farther than he'd guessed and working to catch up. He eased off on his speed and waited, often glancing back, but when another five minutes passed and he still made out no sign of him, he picked up speed and banked.

The wreckage was half hidden in a gully. The pilot almost missed it. Then he saw the horses just below the gully's rim, and, swooping down, causing the horses to pull at their rock-tied reins, he saw his partner climb up from the gully, other men beside him, then the wreckage, and his partner waving at him. The pilot made another sweep, this time low enough to make sure that the other men weren't Mexican, that his partner was apparently all right and waving at him, not in recognition but to tell him to go on—and anyway the ground was too rock-broken to risk landing, so he made another sweep, and, satisfied, he waved and tipped his wings and left them.

🁢🁢🁢🁢🁢 27 🁢🁢🁢🁢🁢

HE made it down to Pershing by late afternoon.

This was the third day of the expedition, March 18, and since the Columbus column was only halfway to the rendezvous, he figured Pershing would still be quite a distance off as well. Indeed, he counted on it. He and his partner had left earlier than scheduled and had pushed hard to get down there so they would have a day or two before they'd have to work. Colonia Dublán was supposed to be some kind of wonder, trees and streams and cultivated fields, a colony of Mormons who were waiting anxiously for signs of help. As the first man down there, he was figuring on quite a welcome, food and drink and generous hospitality, nights spent on a cool porch sleeping, days spent on a bench off from the sun.

Now, the sun down to his right, the pilot saw the country start to change, from rocks and breaks and sweeps of sand

and cactus to green fields and high full trees ahead and running water glinting in the sun. Among the trees he made out tips of houses, some flat-roofed, others pitched and gabled, white from what he guessed was painted wood, still others brown from adobe. He made out rock-piled walls between the fields, well-plowed rows of what he guessed was sprouting corn. He saw the pinpoint figure of a farmer down there, working with a burro and a plow. Up ahead, the stream was bigger now, women by it washing clothes. He saw a horse-drawn wagon moving slowly down a road, then a car, a truck, tents, soldiers, grazing horses, and he realized that Pershing had beat him to it.

☐☐☐☐☐ **28** ☐☐☐☐☐

THE pilot was swearing to himself all the time he came in for a landing.

A lieutenant stood there waiting for him. "Pershing wants to see you."

"Sure he does. Of course he does."

The pilot followed past tents and wagons toward the shelter of some trees. He'd never met the man before, tall, thin, weary-looking, hollow-cheeked, a salt-and-pepper mustache. Pershing was sitting on a gas can, talking to some officers. "I want you west of here," he told the pilot, pointing at a map. "I've sent three columns south and east and west, and I want you with the west. You fly ahead, scout for them, and bring back daily messages to me.''

''I'm afraid I won't be able to do that, sir.''

Pershing frowned and stared at him.

''You'd better send me to the south. There's mountains to the west. I can't fly over them.''

''You can't do *what*?''

''With Jennie, I can do four thousand feet in still air, one thousand if there's wind, but wind means mountains and anyway those mountains look more like ten thousand feet. I'd never make it.''

Pershing kept staring at him.

''You see, sir, Jennie's not too good. If the government would give us something like those Blériots or Martins that the French and English use against the Germans, everything'd be all right. But not with Jennie. No, sir, not with Jennie.''

Pershing stared harder.

''Those Washington . . . Christ, we gave the world the airplane, and we don't even have an air force as good as Japan's.''

He pursed his lips and shook his head.

🎞🎞🎞🎞🎞 **29** 🎞🎞🎞🎞🎞

ONE truck had a broken axle. Another had steam coming from its radiator. It was just as well that the column had

to stop. There was a village up ahead, and Calendar was riding up to check on it. Two other scouts were splitting up to check the flanks. From far back, through the glasses, it had seemed all right, just villagers, no Mexican soldiers, a town that by comparison with what they'd seen so far was big, three hundred buildings, maybe more, a main road going through. Calendar followed the road, hard-baked dirt beneath his horse's hooves, glancing at the buildings on both sides. When he had seen it through the glasses, there had been a lot of motion, people on the street, burros at the front of buildings. Halfway there, the motion had been less, and as he entered, there was hardly anyone. A few men stood in front of doorways, squinting at him. The rest were all inside. The windows had no glass, just squares of wood that could be swung shut from the inside, and now he saw them swinging closed, saw doors swing shut as well. Ahead, a long-haired, round-faced little girl stood in a doorway, looking curiously at him, as an arm from in there grabbed her and slammed the door. From up and down the street Calendar heard the muffled sound of latches snapping shut. One man spat beside his horse's hooves as he rode past. Someone threw a rock. Calendar looked, but there was no one.

He couldn't blame them. After all, there wasn't any way they could win. For years they'd learned that strangers just meant trouble. Either Villa's men would come through and strip the place, or else the federals would. It was true that Villa had in better times provisioned towns like this, stealing cattle from big ranches, dressing out the meat and giving it to peasants, but that was in exchange for loyalty, and whether the strangers going through were handing out or taking, the peasants understood that the hand that gave could take, and the hand that took could come and take again. In the end, they kept to themselves and trusted no one.

It wasn't new to Calendar. He had seen it many times—out west, toward the end of the Indian Wars, neutral tribes as fearful of marauding bands as they were of whites, wanting only to be left alone; in Cuba and the Philippines, any place where the guerrillas lived off locals. As friendly as they tried to be, the neutrals got in trouble from both sides and ended up a special kind of enemy. They could be as dangerous as the people you were after. Even though in theory you were there to help them, you didn't trust them. If they gave you cause, neutral or not, you cut them down.

Now, not wanting to make them nervous, Calendar rode with one hand near his hidden shoulder holster rather than his pistol. There was no way he could cover front and back of him. That was why he'd sent three other scouts to follow up the first two and himself, his own man fifty yards behind, the scout's only job to check for anyone who might step out after Calendar had gone by and try to shoot him. There were hardly any people at all, the buildings getting larger, from huts to sheds to major dwellings, square, flat-roofed, made of brick adobe, pebbles and straw showing in the brown clay, support beams sticking out from upper sides. He looked down alleys, saw occasional burros and scurries of people ducking out of sight, looked ahead and saw the village square, a brick-rimmed well directly in the center, an old man wearing rope-soled sandals and a hemp serape sitting there, and he guessed if there'd be trouble, it was here.

Calendar rode directly over, said hello, the peasant nod-

ding without looking at him, and getting off, the horse between the peasant and himself, Calendar led it to the well. There was a wooden bucket that he was afraid would have some water in it. He didn't think they would poison their own well, but they might put poison in the bucket, and just to be careful he would have to dump it. All the same, water was a precious thing out here, and if the bucket wasn't poisoned, he would be insulting them by dumping it, so he was just as glad to see that it was empty. He lowered it by a rope to a level that in the darkness of the well looked to be twenty feet below, and, hoisting it, he poured the water in a nearby trough and eased off on the horse's reins to let it drink. As soon as he was sure that the water was all right, he reached inside his saddle bag, pushed aside the revolver that was there, took a cup and dipped it in the bucket, drank the water in there he had saved, and thanked the old man for his hospitality.

The old man nodded once again. Still he didn't look at Calendar.

Then glancing over at his backup man who was waiting by the entrance to the square, Calendar reached up his hand, and the backup man rode off across the square. The town was bigger than he first had thought, more like six hundred buildings than three, but the number on this side of town looked less than on the other. Even so, Calendar didn't breathe much until he saw his partner make it all the way down the continuation of the road and join up with the remaining pairs of scouts who had circled the town and were waiting at the other end.

Then, certain now that as long as he was here and on his feet no one would tamper with the well, knowing that the scouts would go to the column and have the major send

a crew for water, Calendar pushed back his hat, remarked to the old man about the heat, stood with his side protected by his horse, and waited.

30

THE column camped a hundred yards away on the other side of town. Its orders had been clear: not to interfere with locals unless there was no other choice. In this case, the water made it necessary. They had been depending on the trucks to return to holes and bring back water as they needed it, but this was the first time trucks were used for that, and no one had counted on the damage that the roads would do: burned-out bearings, overheated radiators, ruptured tires, bent suspensions, oil pans scoured by rocks until their seals were cracked and broken. Sometimes oil spilled out as fast as they could pour it in. They needed water, mostly for the trucks and horses—the men could manage for themselves, cut down on their intake if they had to—and while they had another day's supply, they didn't want to take a chance on some emergency. They took what the well could stand and not go dry, leaving plenty for the village, seeking out the village's mayor and giving him a voucher. This was worthless inasmuch as it had to be redeemed across the border and the mayor likely hadn't been that far from the village all his life, but it was easier

than bringing money, and anyway what good was money in a village based on trade.

Now with sunset nearly on them, the soldiers arranged the trucks and wagons in a circle, guards patrolling the perimeter, picket lines established, horses tethered, troopers taking off their horses' bridles, bits, and saddles, grooming them. Prentice waited until the sun was nearly down before he brought a sawed-off gas can, filling it with water.

"That's enough now," he told his horse. "You'll get sick."

In a while he poured a little more. Then he hitched a feed bag to the horse's head and waited while it ate. This was Army-issue grain that he was giving it. Even so, the expedition had been mustered in a hurry, and he didn't want to go away and risk some pebbles mixed in with the grain, the horse rejecting it. If there were, he'd have to dump the bag and show the horse that he was bringing fresh, checking much more carefully for pebbles, hoping that the horse would not reject this new batch too. As things worked out, the grain was fine, and once the horse had eaten well, Prentice brushed it down once more, and, satisfied that he had done his best, he tended to himself.

Unlike later expeditions where mess tents were put up and separate companies made meals for the rest, these soldiers were forced to make meals for themselves. Mostly the meals were in the form of rations issued them on the first day of the march—beans and dried beef, hardtack, bacon, coffee—which they carried with them and replenished from supply trucks as they went. Their packs were overloaded as a consequence, and while the soldiers had the choice of packing even more in case of trouble, the food itself had little nutritional value, chosen mostly for its bulk. Then too it didn't spoil, and, since its taste was poor, it lasted. Now, his thighs scraped red, his spine and buttocks aching from the months he'd been away from riding, Prentice stooped, his legs splayed in pain, and fumbled in his saddle bag. He sucked a piece of hardtack while he took out sugar, coffee, and beef, walking weak-kneed toward the sergeant and some troopers.

They were crouched in a circle, working hard to start a fire. In the settling darkness, Prentice made out through the space between their legs the flash of matches, wondering what they had found to use for fuel. Dead and sun-baked mesquite branches he saw, coming up to them, bits and pieces from the mesquite built up in a pile, a hollow in there where the sergeant struck another match. It flared and died. The sergeant struck another, then another, and the mesquite pieces slowly caught, edges curling, turning gray, bright flames growing, spreading, lighting up the ground around their boots. The sergeant added other pieces, working up in size. The flames caught these as well, the sergeant adding more until he'd used up one whole bush.

It didn't do much good. The mesquite didn't burn long to begin with, and they only had two other bushes, everyone in camp scouring the ground nearby for what there was. In the cold that settled with the darkness, it gave some heat but not enough to cook with, and the best they could do was crowd around and warm their hands. Ten minutes, and the bushes and the fire were gone.

Prentice went back near the picket line of horses, sitting by his saddle, shifting his pistol so its holster lay along his upper thigh, unhitched his canteen from his belt, and, setting down his cup, he poured some water in it. Then he spooned sugar from his packet, stirred it with the water, bit a piece of beef and chewed it, chewed it more, then as he swallowed, took a drink.

The water had a faint metallic taste. The sugar had no taste to speak of, one sure sign he needed it. Like the rocksalt he'd been sucking on and off all day. As soon as he could taste the salt, he knew that he had had enough and waited. Now he sipped the sweetless sugared water, biting off another piece of beef, and watched the camp around him.

There were troopers standing, wrapped in blankets, shivering. Some were pounding tent pegs, but the ground was solid, and they stopped. Others simply lay down where their saddles were, shifting rocks beneath them, heads upon their packs. A few men still had fires going, less flames all the while, sitting by them, biting at a biscuit or a piece of meat. "Christ," Prentice heard some distance to his right, the loudest voice he'd heard so far—in contrast with their spirit at the start, the other soldiers still and quiet, just too tired for much talk.

He sipped more sugared water, tasting a little sweetness now, thinking, heard two horses nicker near him, swallowed the mulch of beef and biscuit in his mouth, made up his mind, and stood. Across from him he dimly made out, black against the gray of night, the shape of trucks that curved around to form part of the camp's perimeter. He heard the clatter of a side hood being lifted. Then someone lit a lantern, and he saw three yellow-shaded drivers looking at an engine, one among them reaching in to point at something. Five trucks down, another lantern showed two drivers jacking up a wheel and looking under.

He scanned across the camp that way, first to his right until he reached the horses, then back to his left, and he didn't see what he wanted. There were stars but no moon yet, and even with the lanterns and the dwindling glow of fires, there wasn't light enough to make out any detail. The best thing, he decided, was to walk around the rim and, if he had to, crisscross through the camp.

He didn't have to. Starting to his left, forty yards around, just where the wagons ended and the trucks began, he found the old man sitting with his back against a wagon wheel, his legs stretched out, his elbow on his saddle, working on a cigarette. There was the dying flicker of a fire nearby, reaching far enough to show the motion of the old man's hands, but even if there hadn't been, Prentice believed he would have spotted him.

Prentice had been thinking about Calendar for quite a while, not just from when Calendar had saved his life but from something the sergeant had said also, and now Prentice stood there, blending with the darkness, waiting, mustering himself while Calendar's big hands deftly rolled the cigarette and raised it to his lips to lick it. Still Prentice waited, watching as the old man held it firmly and sealed it, turned the whole thing in his mouth to wet it all around, then studied it, and looked out at the darkness toward him.

"Lord, don't tell me. You haven't come to thank me again."

Prentice almost walked away. Not that he hadn't been expecting a conversation like the one that he'd been through in the storeroom. Indeed, he'd prepared for it, had braced himself for it. But he had thought that he had come unnoticed, and all the while the old man had been conscious of him, and, once again, in the old man's presence he felt foolish.

Prentice checked his impulse and stepped forward, stopping by his boots.

"No. I've come to ask you something."

"Ask me what?"

Prentice waited, uncertain now if he should carry on. "To teach me."

"Teach you what?"

"All this."

"I don't know what you mean."

The old man wouldn't give an inch. He turned away and lit the cigarette. In the harsh flame in the dark, the furrows of his face looked deep against his leathered skin. Thin, grizzled hair and stubbled cheeks. He looked as if he had aged another ten years.

"Of course you do, but let me tell you anyway," Prentice said. "When I signed on and they trained me, they worked with me on handguns, rifles, and machine guns, but the first two I knew pretty well already, and I knew more than enough about horses to begin with, so they put me through formations and they gave me books to read and they said that once I got to a permanent camp, experience would be the best teacher."

"And they were right."

"That's fine if all you've got to do is sit around and watch all day, but Columbus was for real. And so is this. The next time something like that happens, and for sure it's going to happen, I can't count on somebody like you around to save me."

The old man nodded, drawing on his cigarette. The tip

glowed in the dark. "You knew the risks. If you didn't like them, what the hell did you sign on for?"

"Maybe the same reason you did."

"I don't think so." It was a mistake, and Prentice instantly regretted it, the old man leaning forward, glaring at him. "Don't presume, boy."

Prentice shook his head. "You're right. I'm sorry."

"You damn well should be. I won't have any fresh-faced nineteen-, twenty-year-old kid coming around thinking how he understands me. 'Cause you don't understand a thing, boy. Not a thing. Do you follow me? Do you understand that much anyhow?"

"Yes, sir, I do. That's why I'm here."

Prentice hoped the "sir" would help, and indeed the old man seemed to weaken, stubbing out his cigarette and thinking.

"And anyway why should I teach you? Assuming it can be taught."

"No reason I guess."

"That's right."

And that was that. It hadn't helped at all. The old man turned to make another cigarette, and clearly he expected him to go. Prentice moved to turn and then thought better.

"Except maybe this. You're sixty-five years old. You've seen every kind of action this country has been in since the Civil War and right now this minute the Germans have submarines cruising the Atlantic."

"What's *that* supposed to mean?"

"You're the last. I don't think anybody's fooling themselves what we're doing down here. Villa's just an excuse. This is all a dress rehearsal for when we go overseas, and once we do, your kind of life is over, everything you know is useless. You've got what, maybe ten, fifteen good years left and then you're gone and everything you know is gone with you. What I'm offering is a chance for you to pass it on.''

The old man moved as if to speak and Prentice cut him off.

"I know. Once this is over, if I live, it's not going to do me any good either, so there's no sense in trying to appeal to you on that point either. But there's this too. Like with my father's farm or what used to be his farm until the city finally spread so far out that it swallowed the place up and my father took an apartment and I signed on with the Army. Everything's changing, and I'm just enough of a dumb clod-kicking farmboy at heart to want to keep some of the old ways with me.''

"Are you through now?''

"Yes.'' Prentice nodded.

"All right then, let me tell you something. And you listen hard because it'll be the only damn thing you ever hear me try to teach you. You're not the first. I've had them all, a whole bright eager endless string of them, right through the last of the Indian Wars and Cuba and the rest, right on up to here, and they all looked like you and they all sounded just like you and they all had the one same thing at heart, to stay alive. And I told them no just like I told you. Because if you want to stay alive, so do I, and once you commit yourself to somebody you start looking out for them almost as much as you do for yourself, and that's how a man gets killed. . . . It's like I don't work with Indians because I fought against them once and now I still get nervous knowing they're behind me. It's like people say I don't make friends and that's just fine with me because friends make me nervous knowing they're ahead of me. There's only one rule. Look out for yourself and don't let anything or anyone distract you. You remember that, and you'll do fine. Just fine. Now I'm tired. I've got a watch to stand in a few hours and I want to get some sleep.''

This last came out so quickly that it seemed the topic hadn't even changed direction. The old man stood and grabbed a blanket by his saddle, wrapping it around him. He looked once more at Prentice, then lay down by the wagon wheel. Prentice waited, but the old man's eyes were shut, and in a while Prentice slowly turned and walked away.

The men were still and quiet as he passed among them toward his saddle and his gear. By now the cold was chilling, and he huddled in his blanket like the rest, looking around the camp, the horses calm, the drifting shapes of sentries pacing the perimeter. He glanced at the old man, then over at the one remaining fire, curious how anyone had kept it going for so long, but it was dwindling now, smaller and lower, one last flicker, then a glow, and it was out.

▣▣▣▣▣ 31 ▣▣▣▣▣

DAWN was even colder. There was ice in canteens, dippers frozen over, troopers chipping at the ice with knives, then rubbing their hands to keep them warm. Over by the grain trucks, stretched out in his blanket, the major was still asleep. Calendar knelt and put his hand on his shoulder. The major started, looking at him, frowning.

"I think you'd better see," Calendar said.

The major didn't ask. Calendar just kept looking at him. Then Calendar waved for him to follow, and the major, crawling from his blanket, looked out where the old man pointed past the grain trucks toward the desert side of camp. There was a solid line of horsemen, too far out to tell their uniforms or the details of the banners some were holding, but the major seemed to know even as he asked if they were federals.

The old man nodded, sucking at his lips. "They must have been camped close by in a draw. That's not all. Look over here."

The old man waved the major toward the other side of camp, passing troopers who had stopped what they were doing and were standing, pointing, talking, clear that word had gotten around to them as well. They reached the wagons on the other side of camp and looked out toward the town. A solid line of villagers, holding sticks and clubs, was at the outskirts, staring toward the camp.

"Those federals must have been busy all night organizing. I'll say that for them," the old man told the major. "It's my fault. I should have been out there checking."

"Never mind that. Let's just get out of here. Lieutenant, muster the column!"

🔳🔳🔳🔳🔳 32 🔳🔳🔳🔳🔳

IT took them fifteen minutes to do what normally took an hour, not even seeing to the horses, those that hadn't been fed would have to wait, just saddling them, packing equipment, starting trucks, clipping teams onto wagons.

The old man cinched his saddle and watched the column start to form, trucks moving so there was a space to go through, soldiers mounting up and riding out. Soon wagons would peel off and follow, moving in a line, followed by the trucks and other riders.

Calendar looked. The villagers began to move the moment that the column did. They were ready with their sticks and clubs, and now that Calendar looked closer, he could see bright uniforms among them and in back of them, federals who were giving them directions. The federals must have gone in late at night and roused them, told them what to do, and likely forced them. There were children mixed in with the line and women too, and for good reason. If the column wanted first of all to keep away from trouble with the federals, it wanted even more to stay clear of the villagers. Dead soldiers would be one thing, dead civilians quite another, and the federals were counting on that, using the villagers to force the column to break camp, pushing them to force the column to move faster.

33

PRENTICE mounted up and started forward with his company and, as he did, felt something strike him. He touched his shoulder. To his right he saw a rock go by, and looking back he saw the villagers stooping, grabbing rocks, and throwing them. The column moved a little faster.

Up ahead the federals were waiting. The front of the column angled to the left to work around them, and the federals split up, one-half riding far off to the left to flank them. Looking back, Prentice saw that the villagers had stopped now, the column totally moved out and in a line, working slowly forward. He looked ahead and saw the column riding through the space provided by the federals. The Mexican soldiers stayed about a hundred yards away on either side, and once the column was partway through, they started moving with it, their tall thin leader staring from the right. The major must have ordered it: Prentice saw the head of the column change its rhythm, troopers riding quicker, a space between one group of horsemen and another as the troopers down the line sped up to fill it in, a space that like a ripple continued down the line until the men ahead of him were riding faster and he picked up speed to fill the space in and the men behind him worked to follow. The federals picked up speed as well. Prentice wondered what was going on, whether the federals meant to attack, or whether this was just intimidation. Whatever, it was working. They had forced the column to behave defensively. The federals had control.

34

CALENDAR came riding past to speed the column's progress as it changed from trot to canter. There was dust among the horses, everything difficult to see, but just for a moment Prentice made out up ahead the draw between two low-slung hills that they were heading for. The federals were matching them on both sides as the column hurried forward, and Prentice never knew which side the first shot came from, American or federal, whether it was aimed or just a signal. He wasn't even sure he'd heard it till he heard another, and another, and suddenly both sides were firing openly. A man ahead of him was falling from his horse, a second farther on. Prentice had no choice. Later he would be surprised that at the time he didn't even think about it. He just drew his pistol, aimed at the federals to his left, and fired. Impossible to see if in the dust and distance he connected, but he fired again and then again, kicking at his horse to keep up with the others as the draw ahead loomed closer.

□□□□□ **35** □□□□□

THEY were galloping, the column losing order, what had been four men abreast turned into eight and sometimes ten, firing, rushing forward. The federals were charging closer on both sides. Even if they wanted to, they had no other choice. The slopes on both sides were so close that the federals had to narrow. Up ahead the column reached the draw, and Prentice saw a line of troopers pull away to stop and get off, kneeling with their rifles. They were firing past the column toward the federals. Prentice passed them, riding up the draw, dust rising all around him as he squinted to control his horse and get up toward the exit.

□□□□□ **36** □□□□□

THEY were bunched together, forced to crowd one another by the narrow slopes on both sides. Prentice heard men screaming, shots behind him. The dust got thicker. He kicked his horse, and suddenly he burst out into the open, a half-mile dusty basin all around him, rimmed by gentle rising slopes, the column heading straight across and spreading out, more shots close behind him. Up ahead, a little to the left, he saw the old man falling.

37

SOMETHING yanked at him. Calendar felt his sleeve rip open, bloody, and before he knew it, toppled, landing so hard that he didn't feel it, body rolling, flopping, ending on his back, the sky above him, blinking while the pain rushed in on him. He'd lost some time. He didn't know how much. He fought to clear his head and sit and stand, falling back, cursing until he made it. He looked around. His horse was gone, the column charging past. He looked for where he'd dropped his gun but couldn't find it, grabbed the revolver in its shoulder holster, and fired at the federals looming toward him. Dimly recognizing the kid he had helped as the kid rode past, Calendar fired again and started running.

He tripped and landed on his wounded shoulder, wincing, struggling to his feet. The slopes were too far off. He couldn't make it.

Up ahead, he saw a trooper swing around and gallop back the way he'd come. He couldn't figure what the trooper was doing.

Then he saw: The trooper was the kid.

And realized: The kid was coming back for him.

Calendar was a moment adjusting. Then he turned and shot to give the kid some cover. At once he looked back to see the kid charging closer.

The kid was hunched down, firing past the horse's head, coming to a line of rocks and vaulting it, the horse not even missing stride as it came down, lunging forward. The old man had to marvel at it, the ease with which the kid had done it. He fired to give the kid more cover, waiting, braced to swing up as the kid went right on past, and the old man didn't understand that either. Then he saw the kid rein around and come back toward him once again, and realized. The kid knew horses every bit as much as he'd let on, the strain the horse would feel if it turned racing with two men, the time they'd lose the longer they rode double. Now the kid was close upon him, barely stopping as he reached to help the old man up and kicked the horse to get away.

They galloped awkwardly across the basin. Ahead, the column was spread out and charging toward the slopes. Behind, very close, were the federals. Gunshots echoed through the basin.

🎞️🎞️🎞️🎞️🎞️ **38** 🎞️🎞️🎞️🎞️🎞️

THE old man saw his horse and nudged the kid and told him. It was running among a group of troopers, its stirrups bouncing as it fled. The old man told the kid once again, and reining gently, angling toward it, the kid came closer, then beside it, reaching to grab the reins and slow it, slow it more, the old man waiting until the horse was nearly stopped, then slipping from the saddle, stumbling, grabbing at the reins and saddle horn with one hand while the horse lurched forward, nearly dragging him as he fumbled for the stirrup, climbing up. The old man's left arm was in agony. He kicked his horse and galloped forward, the federals shooting behind him.

He saw that the major was in charge again, the trucks and wagons spread out in a line. Troopers fired from behind the vehicles. They fired from the slopes and from the top as well, off their horses, on their knees or stomachs, firing, aiming, firing. The old man galloped past them, working up the hill, dismounting, running with his horse.

▯▯▯▯▯▯ 39 ▯▯▯▯▯▯

PRENTICE was before him, shooting toward the basin, working the bolt on his rifle, aiming, firing. He saw the old man stumble toward the top, still clutching the reins of his horse as he made it up and fell down gasping, his shoulder bloody, caked with dust. Prentice fought the impulse to go over and instead shot toward the basin. A federal dropped where he'd been aiming, but he couldn't tell whose bullet had hit him. The next time Prentice looked over, the old man was still lying there.

Prentice shot again, and now the fight had changed, the federals in retreat, or what at first he thought was one. They rode back to the middle of the basin and regrouped, and now he saw what they were doing: a mounted charge. The federals spread out in a line, the tall thin leader in the middle, starting slowly forward as someone near Prentice shouted to cease fire.

Prentice looked. It was the major. The major shouted it again, a lieutenant and a sergeant shouting it as well. The troopers checked themselves, a few still getting off some shots but most just lowering their rifles and staring toward the basin as the line down there moved slowly forward.

Prentice turned: The old man had sat up and was pulling out a handkerchief. The old man tied it just below his shoulder, just above the blood, holding one end with his teeth and knotting it. Then he stood and looked down at the line of horsemen moving slowly toward them. The muscles of his face were working as he touched his shoulder, turned, and pulled his rifle from its scabbard.

"Miles!" the major said.

"Some bastard down there owes me!"

"It's too far!"

But the old man wouldn't listen. He looked down at his rifle, checking it. It had the longest barrel Prentice had ever seen, and he was flipping the lever so a round was in the chamber, untying his saddle bags and setting them on the top of the slope. Everyone was watching.

He lay down, wincing, steadying the barrel on his saddle bags.

The line down there moved slowly closer, hard to tell in the sun's glare and the dust how far, two hundred yards at least, the men down there like tiny figures in a game.

The old man squinted, aiming, wiped his eyes, and squinted once again. He fumbled in his saddle bags, pulled out a pair of steel-rimmed glasses, slipped them on, and aimed again. Prentice held his breath.

Even with the saddle bags, the old man had to put his wounded arm forward, hand against the grip. He cursed and shook his head, then eased his finger on the trigger, squeezing, and the shot was like a cannon going off, recoil jolting, the old man going with it as he lay spread where he was and waited.

After what seemed a second, an invisible hand flicking at a toy, the tall thin leader down there toppled smoothly from his horse. It must have been the distance. He seemed to take a long time falling.

Troopers cheered.

The line down there pulled up, staring from their fallen leader toward the top.

"That'll do it," the old man said. "It lends us time, and once we're set up here, they'll have to give this up."

The old man braced himself, drew up his legs to kneel, and stood. "From the looks of their next-in-command down there, the one who's doing all the talking, he doesn't want the responsibility anyhow."

And Calendar was right. One man down there seemed to be talking quite a lot, gesturing with his hands while someone got down off his horse and checked the fallen officer. Riders came in from the flanks. The line was breaking up.

"Your arm," the major said.

"It isn't broken."

"Well, at least that's something."

"Sure."

And Prentice had to smile. The way the old man stood there, glasses on his nose, rifle in one hand, blood dripping from the other, dust from head to foot, it was like he wasn't even mindful of his wounded arm as he stared down toward the basin at the federals splitting into groups, some milling around their fallen leader, others riding off to get their wounded and their dead.

The sound of shots was ringing in his ears. Prentice looked down at his hands, and they were shaking.

He had to smile. So much had happened, he hadn't even thought about himself.

He'd done all right.

◻◻◻◻◻ **40** ◻◻◻◻◻

THEY reached camp two days later, straggling in near sunset. The men of Pershing's column who were there waiting for them couldn't quite believe it. There were wounded on stretchers and on the wagons and the trucks, troopers with bandages around their heads, others with blood-spattered thighs, slumped forward painfully, holding their stomachs as they rode, a long slow procession of agony and exhaustion. One horse simply gave out, its front legs buckling, toppling forward as its rider slipped clear, giving out himself, his knees bending, slumping to the dirt. The rest were staring forward toward the village and its trees. All that green and shade and coolness, at that moment it seemed about the most beautiful thing they had ever hoped to see, and in the midst of their horses' clomping, the jingling of equipment, the rattle of motors, they just kept staring straight ahead, silent.

Then they reached the trees, and there were more men coming over, staring at them as they plodded past the tents and horses and the wagons of the other column's bivouac, the buildings of the town far off across from them, toward the section of the camp that was assigned to them. They crossed a hollow-rumbling wooden bridge, a deep cool-looking stream beneath it, faces changing as they saw the water, the sergeant stopping two as they slid from their horses, starting toward it.

"Hey!" the sergeant told them. It was like a growl, the sergeant pointing toward their horses, and they knew exactly what he meant. It didn't matter that they'd broken ranks, it mattered that they'd thought about themselves before their mounts, the two men nodding weakly, walking slowly back to grab their horses' reins and follow where the column had pulled up and started to disperse.

🎞🎞🎞🎞🎞 **41** 🎞🎞🎞🎞🎞

SOMEONE rigged a picket line.

Prentice unsaddled his horse, unhitching the bridle, slipping on a halter, tying the rope to the picket line. He patted the horse, talking to it, wiping off its flecks of sweat.

Among the cool, sun-shut-out trees, the air felt calm and soothing, the sounds around him muffled by the soft absorbent earth. After the stones and gravel of the desert, the ground here almost had a spring to it, making him light-footed, the horse he worked on pawing at the ground and sniffing, its hoof striking with a hollow thump. He brushed the horse down, pausing to unstick his heavy woolen shirt from where his sweat was cooling on his chest, looked over at the stream and then at where the sun was almost down, brushed the horse some more, and dreamed of food and rest, forcing himself to wait until the horse was cool enough so he could feed and water it and then look after himself.

Over by the stream, quite a ways down but not so far that he couldn't distinguish, he saw the old man walking. Calendar had evidently finished with his horse, moving slowly, his head bent, one leg working better than the other, his left arm in a sling, toward the bank. The old man stooped and braced himself to ease down toward the water. The next thing, he was out of sight.

🔲🔲🔲🔲🔲 42 🔲🔲🔲🔲🔲

CALENDAR didn't even bother taking off his boots, just set them in the water, letting it soak his pants around his legs and funnel past his socks to the bottom of his feet. At first his feet were numb, but then the temperature of the water changed until it matched his body, and the stream felt cool and soothing. He lay back on the grassy slope and looked up at the dimming sky.

In a moment he heard someone walk along the bank and stop above him. He didn't bother seeing who it was, just out of habit reached beneath his vest to touch his shoulder holster, looking toward the sky. He hoped whoever it was up there would go away. Instead he heard grass shifting behind him, felt vibrations under him as someone scampered down the slope and settled to his right. He didn't look.

"For what it's worth"—it was the major—"Pershing's going to let the Thirteenth on its own. We'll be cutting west, then south along the mountains."

The old man nodded, looking at the sky. There was a cloud up there, the only cloud in sight, drifting almost over him, one edge tinted red against the sunset-yellowed sky. The thought of Pershing took him back. "How is he?"

"Mad as hell."

The old man laughed.

43

MAD wasn't quite the word. Furious was more like it. Pershing had been showing off the touring car that he had rented from a Mormon, when the major brought him news of the attack. This was the famous open Dodge that Pershing would lead the expedition in, and he had put the top down, one door open, a group of officers and correspondents with him all the time he listened, saying "Hell!" as he slammed the door. "If those damned Washington politicians won't see to it that we get some cooperation down here, I'm going to put some pressure on to make them. You gentlemen have my permission to write anything you want about this incident. The only thing I ask is to see your copy, not to censor it but to guarantee it's extra strong. I want every stateside newspaper to carry this story and I want everyone who reads that story to get in touch with Washington. By the time we're through, Mexico City's going to have cooperation shoved down its throat."

This wasn't Pershing's standard practice. Normally he kept tight control on what reporters said about him. Later, in the First World War, all reporters traveling with him would have to post ten thousand dollars bond, and if they smuggled stories past a censor, Pershing would confiscate the bond and in one case he almost charged a man with treason.

Now the sudden easement of his policy seemed to brighten the reporters. A few were smiling. Indeed, now that Pershing had finished talking and had thought about it, he seemed to brighten too, looking at the major, walking over to his tent, and reaching past the flaps to grab at something.

"Here, Major, I think you could use a bit of this."

He held up a whiskey bottle and a cup.

"With the general's permission, after you," the major said.

The general looked at him and smiled.

"With my permission, after all of us."

He reached in for other cups, the correspondents coming close, holding empty cans, the lids off canteens, anything that was around. Pershing poured into them, then everyone waited until the general was finished.

He straightened, raised his cup, and looked at them.

"To Villa, the son of a bitch, and wherever we catch up to him."

"Hear, hear," they toasted, lifting cups and glasses before they drank.

🎞 44 🎞

Two troopers ran stark naked down the bank and leaped into the stream. The major watched as they landed, splashing. "I guess you knew about his family being killed."

It was the first time since the major had sat down that the old man looked at him.

"No," he said. "I didn't."

"Sure. Last summer. After Pershing got transferred to El Paso. His family was back in San Francisco packing up to follow. A fire in the night. Killed his wife and three daughters. His young boy was the only one got clear."

The old man looked more intensely at him. Prentice would have recognized the look. It was the same as when the column had set out and the old man watched the major kiss his girl and boy and wife.

The major felt unnerved by the look. "Anyway it's

changed him. He's a little thinner, seems a little older. His temper's the same, but you get the idea it's for different reasons. One of his aides told me he complains a lot more than he used to. Not enough supplies, not enough men, that sort of thing. It's like he's thrown himself into this thing to help him forget and he feels he's going to have to do it on his own because he can't depend on anybody else to help him.''

The old man turned away then, looking toward the stream.

They didn't speak for quite a while, and suddenly the old man stood up awkwardly to go.

45

PRENTICE was sitting against a tree, eating the first good meal of the campaign, a kind of stew that the Mormons had fixed for them. He spooned a chunk of meat and gravy-soaked potato into his mouth, chewing slowly as he looked and saw the old man standing there.

"Don't bother thanking me," Prentice said.

"I'm not about to. It was foolish."

"All the same, we're even."

The old man shrugged. "You were right about knowing horses, that's for sure. I guess the first thing is to get you another handgun."

The last part didn't register. Prentice chewed some

more, then stopped and swallowed, putting down his spoon and plate and squinting toward the old man, wondering if he had just heard right and if it meant what he thought it did.

The old man kept on standing there.

TWO

██████ 46 ██████

GEORGIA, 1864

Word had already reached them about the burning of Atlanta. There were rumors of what the Yankees would do next. The Confederate, General Hood, had pulled back from Atlanta, and many thought that Sherman would go after him. No one thought of what had happened in Virginia or guessed that what had happened once could happen again. Even when the signs were unmistakable, they couldn't quite believe it. Instead of going after Hood or any other military target, Sherman abandoned his supply lines, and, in an effort to demoralize the South, he turned his sixty thousand men around to march directly from Atlanta to Savannah and the sea, destroying or consuming everything along the way.

November, and a good time for it. As one historian later said, ''They moved on a sixty-mile front through a rich land where the harvest was in, the barns were stuffed with corn and forage, smokehouses bulged with hams and bacon, and the fields were full of cattle. Each morning each brigade detached a forage company of about fifty men to comb the countryside a few miles to either side of the brigade's line of march. Seizing farm wagons and carriages, they loaded them with bacon, eggs, cornmeal, chickens, turkeys and ducks, sweet potatoes—whatever could be carried off—and delivered their loads to the brigade commissaries at the end of each day. Meanwhile, other units drove off livestock. What they could not take, they killed. To save ammunition, they sabered pigs and poleaxed horses and mules between the ears. From sunup to sundown lean veterans accustomed to hardtack and salt pork gorged themselves on ham and yams and fresh beef, and as they advanced across the state they grew fat and sleek. So did the Negroes to whom they gave the plantation masters' food, and who frolicked on the heels of the advancing host in the living embodiment of the famous ditty:

Say Darkies has you seen old Massa
Wid de muffstache on his face
Go long de road sometime dis mornin'
Like he gwine to leave da place?

De Massa run, ha-ha!
De Darkey stay, ho-ho!
I tink it must be Kingdom Coming
And de Year ob Jubilo.

"It was indeed the Year of Jubilo for the Negroes, just as for Sherman's laughing veterans the march had become a picnic promenade. From wing to wing sixty miles apart there rose columns of smoke as the advancing army trailed its own somber clouds of destruction. Warehouses, bridges, barns, machine shops, depots and factories were burned. Not even houses were spared, especially not by the 'bummers,' those deserters, desperadoes and looters, North and South, who were drawn to the march for the sake of loot. These were the men who forced old men and helpless women to divulge the secret places where silver, jewelry and money were hidden. They danced with muddy, hobnailed boots on snow-white linen or gleaming table tops, smashing furniture with gun butts, slashing feather beds with sabers and shattering windows and mirrors with empty bottles. Sherman, who might have restrained them, did little to stop them. 'War is cruelty, and you cannot refine it,' he had told the people of Atlanta, and it was his intention to demonstrate that the Confederacy was powerless to protect its people against it.''

Their farm was in the middle of the state, directly in the line of march, although they didn't know that until it was too late. One morning there were looters in the barn. His father tried to stop them, and they shot him. His mother ran out toward him, and they shot her too. They raped his sister, shot her, disemboweled his brother with a saber, took the horses and the pigs, shot the dog, burned the barn and house, and rode off with the wagon filled with food and grain.

The youngest, thirteen years old, he had seen it, some of it, from the top floor of the house. He had been asleep when it began, and roused had gotten up, squinting out the bedroom window just in time to see his father fall, his mother close behind.

Starting down the stairs, he'd seen two soldiers struggling with his sister. Another soldier, coming up the stairs, had clubbed him with a gun butt. He had awakened in the smoke and flames, stumbling down the stairs and out to the porch, remembering his sister, going back in, seeing her on the sofa, her dress above her neck, her undergarments ripped and bloody, a red stain at her chest, his mutilated brother on the floor nearby, the flames already starting on them. Coughing, moving toward them, he had held his hands up, forced back by the heat, a timber falling, then another, blocking him. He'd tried another way, the flames there even stronger, roaring, other timbers falling, his clothes on fire, his brother and sister out of sight, the fire now all before him as he stumbled back and thrashed to get his clothes off, banging through the door and rolling on the ground. His neck stung, and his head, his hair on fire, beating at it. Then the flames were out, and he was lying there, his singed hair in his hands, the stench upon him, the fire roaring even louder, its heat waves rolling over him. He crawled a little, crawled a little more. Still the heat kept burning him. He grabbed his mother and his father, dragging them, stopping past the gateway to the yard. He lay there quite a while.

He knew they were dead. There wasn't any question, their eyes open, their eyes glazed, staring out at nothing. Still he had to check them, but it wasn't any good. He lay there staring at them. Then he stood and saw that the barn had fallen in. The house was nearly gutted. He watched as the roof fell in and then one wall, and everything went blurry on him as he registered that something warm and wet was trickling down his face, that he was crying. He looked around for someone he could hurt. There wasn't anyone. He staggered to the barn and saw that all the feed bins near it had been emptied, that the carriage and the wagon were gone, and stumbling toward the main gate after them, he tripped and realized that he was barefoot, naked.

He glanced back toward his mother and father by the fence where he had dragged them, starting toward them as the three remaining walls caved in. He buried them. He looked around for anything that he could use, grabbed the clothes that he had taken from his father, put them on, rolled up the cuffs of the pants, pulled in the belt, rolled up the sleeves—and with oversized socks on his feet, with leaf-stuffed boots put over them, staring toward the graves, the smoking ruins of the barn and house, he started off.

🞑🞑🞑🞑🞑 47 🞑🞑🞑🞑🞑

IT took him quite a while. At first he didn't know what he was doing. He thought that if he hurried he might catch them. Then he realized that even if he caught them he would have no chance against them. One boy and a half-dozen men. He'd seen that many anyhow. Three inside and three others in the yard. There could be even more. A quick glimpse through the window, another on the stairs, the two down there who'd struggled with his sister, the other coming toward him, beard-stubbled and muddy, tou-sle-haired. He wasn't even sure that he could recognize them. But the wagon and the carriage, those at least he knew, those he could be sure of. He would keep his eyes out for the wagon and the carriage, and anybody with them he would kill.

Not right away, not so that he'd be in any danger. And anyway he wanted to be sure he got them all, so he would wait, and when he found them he would wait some more, and then he'd get them one by one. Maybe he would wait till each was on his own and sleeping, and he'd knife them, or he'd shoot them.

For his sister. For his brother, his mother, his father, the barn, the house. But most of all for himself.

Five miles down the road he found the carriage, a wheel off in a ditch. He had expected that. The wheel had been unsteady. His father had meant to fix it. Now he never would.

He kept going, faster down the road. The leaves had turned to pulp now in his boots, and he was limping badly, walking faster nonetheless. He felt his shins begin to throb. But he kept going.

Then he realized that if he continued like this he would lame himself. Better to get there slowly than not at all. So he removed the clumsy boots and walked in his stockinged feet along the dry grass by the road, and just as well because five minutes later he heard horses and he just had time to hide before a group of Union soldiers rode past. As much as he could tell, a different group. It didn't matter. He saw that they had bulging sacks across their saddles, blood on their clothes. He cursed and followed.

And then he came upon them, hearing them at first, a distant din that grew and grew as he came closer, men and horses, pigs and ducks and turkeys, chickens, all at once together, deafening, every kind of sound that he could think of, coming up a rise and looking down and there they were, an endless sweep of men and horses, livestock, wagons, stretching off as far and wide as he could see, and they were moving, blue and brown and white and every other color, mostly blue though, dust cloud rising, muting them, the soldiers moving, some on horseback, some on foot, what looked like tens of thousands, maybe fifty, sixty thousand, moving, crushing, trampling, like a scourge of locusts, and he knew he'd never find the men he was looking for. He'd try. He might get lucky. But he knew he'd never find them.

He kept going anyhow. He followed all the way. He found a young boy's boots that had been thrown aside. He never knew why they'd been stolen in the first place, but they nearly fit him, just a little big, and grabbing rags that had been thrown away as well, he tied them to his feet as extra socks and put the boots on and they fit him and he kept going. He caught a wind-blown soldier's cap and put it on, shelter from the sun. He found a sack of food. They had so much they didn't care that they had dropped it.

And he kept moving with them, close beside one flank, coughing in the dust, staring at each wagon that went by, falling back, now no longer with them, pacing with the bands of camp followers. They were eating food the troopers had been giving them, singing, laughing, shouting, staring at him, and he moved a distance off, working hard to keep up with the column, and at last it stopped for the night, and he crawled in some bushes, and he slept.

The next day was the same, the next day after that. Each morning as the soldiers rose and ate, he started off ahead of them, trying to gain distance, knowing that by midday he'd be falling back, staring at the wagons, squinting at the troopers' faces, but he didn't see them, and he walked.

He kept walking. He walked until he thought he would drop, and he kept on.

He came to where the soldiers had built bridges on a river, log-raft sections linked with beams and rope, and he was quite a distance back by then. The soldiers had already crossed, a group of sentries at each bridge keeping the camp followers back while the soldiers on the other side began to pull the bridges in. The camp followers started shouting. The soldiers must have tired of them, had enough of feeding them, and wanting to move freely they'd decided to get rid of them, pulling in the bridges while the sentries stood with rifles ready, watching as they moved across the river, pulled in by the soldiers, getting smaller as their section of the bridges moved across.

The camp followers kept on shouting. Some crept toward the river, wading in, the current catching them and swirling them downstream. They fought to swim back to the bank, some never making it. The others just kept shouting.

He moved up the river, looking for a place to cross. There wasn't any.

He found a log down near the water, waded in and pushed, hanging on as it went slowly toward the current, then sped up. The water was cold, tugging at him.

He fought to keep his hold. The log spun, and the next thing he was under, trying to get up, the water all around him. Choking, gagging, he struggled, and the log spun again, and he was able to breathe.

He looked. The bank that he had left was getting smaller. He looked the other way and discovered that he was going downstream in the current. He kicked to aim the log across, but he was going downstream all the same,

102

and he didn't have much choice. He just kept clinging, hoping that the log would get there on its own.

It took him down the river many miles. He didn't know how many, but the time seemed quite a while and he was moving fast, and even then he only reached the other bank because the river curved and the log traveled near the bank. Passing where a piece of land stuck out, he took a chance, let go, and swam and almost didn't make it, but he did.

48

HE almost died that day. It took him many years to understand why. He lay on the sand bank, gasping, sobbing, dripping wet and chilled, and waited for his strength, which never came. He took some soggy bread that he had in his sack and tried to eat it and almost threw up. He knew that he was sick, but he thought that it was just from being tired. He'd heard the word *exposure*, but he'd never understood exactly what it meant, knew people died from it but thought that it was just because they wandered in a blizzard and they froze. He didn't understand how heat could drain from him when he was cold and wet, didn't know that even on a mild day in Georgia in November with a slight wind picking up and chilling him, no way to build a fire, no way to dry his clothes, he could lie on the bank getting weaker and in several hours simply die. It hadn't anything to do with catching cold or getting pneumonia. It was loss of strength from loss of heat.

■□■□■□■□■□ 49 ■□■□■□■□■□

HE got weaker, mumbling to himself, becoming dizzy. He tried to stand and fell back, and the only thing that saved him was his need to catch up to the soldiers. He knew he'd lost a lot of time and distance and that all the while he lay there he was losing more. He tried to move and didn't want to, but he knew he had to, and he braced himself and stood and started up the bank. As near as he could tell, the river had been fairly straight. He figured if he cut off on an angle to his right he would find some sign of where the raiders had gone. Really he would have a hard time missing the trail, that many men and horses and equipment. It was just a question of how long, and he started off, walking slowly, staggering, the socks and rags in his boots now wet and chaffing, causing blisters. He kept on, squinting toward the distance, passing trees and hills and rock-built fences, farms nearby that when he got to them were burned, the people from them lying dead, ignoring them as he kept on, and now he found that he was falling. Once or twice would not have bothered him, but he was falling quite a lot, and now he found as well that he was passing places that he thought he had already passed. He'd gotten turned around, going back the way he'd come, turning once more, sighting on a landmark in the distance, trees or rocks or points of hills, and stumbling toward them. Sighting on another spot and stumbling toward that too, it was a while before he realized that he was where the grass was trampled down, that he'd been in it for some time now, walking in its course. He didn't understand why everything was turning gray on him, and then he realized that the sun was almost gone. He didn't know how long he'd walked. He didn't know how far. He didn't remember hardly any of it, and then, falling in the dark, finding that he could not stand, that he was shivering uncontrollably and retching, he lay in the dirt, staring straight ahead at something that fascinated him until he realized it was a fire and weakly crawled toward it.

They told him later that they almost shot him, a low dark object crawling toward the camp. But then they heard the moaning and they took a chance and watched it come, and it was just a small boy dressed in rags, one hand out before the other, crawling, knees braced, crawling, and he didn't make it to the fire, just stuck out one hand, twenty yards to go, and slumped down in the dirt, and didn't move.

They frowned at him, hesitated, then rushed to see if they could help, picking up his dead weight, moving toward the fire. They found his Union soldier's cap where he had stuck it in his shirt when he went in the river. They stripped him of his clothes and wrapped him in a blanket, warming him beside the fire while they dried his clothes and tried to feed him, hot drinks and a little meat, but he wouldn't touch the meat.

He was still asleep when they set out the next morning. They put him in a wagon, and he didn't wake till noon.

Even then he was delirious, barely drinking, drifting back to sleep, and he didn't really wake till they were camped again. Eating some of what they gave him, he stared at them while they told him how they'd found him, how he had nearly died. They told him too what he had said about a river, and they wondered what had happened to him. He didn't want to talk. He drifted back to sleep, and when he woke up in the night, he was thinking clearly enough to realize that they didn't know about his mother and his father and the rest. They wouldn't trust him if they did. So in the morning he told them that his father was a scrounger who'd abandoned him, that he'd been following the column to get food, had tried to cross the river and had nearly drowned. They looked at him. He couldn't tell if they believed him.

He stayed with them throughout December, moving southeast with the column toward Savannah, hanging back and getting separated, on the outskirts when they took it, then walking in to find what sixty thousand anxious dirty tired men could do to a city. They stripped the saloons and hotels first, breaking anything that stopped them and then breaking just for the sake of breaking, windows, doors, tables, chairs, yanking down sashes, smashing mirrors, soldiers walking down the street with several bottles underneath one arm while they gulped from others. They gutted food stores, kitchens, bakeries. Somewhere in between they started on the women.

He kept looking for the wagon, for the men he had come with, but he couldn't find them. He saw officers who stood on corners, trying to ignore the riot, even joining in. It was obvious that they couldn't stop it even if they wanted to. The purpose of the march was to teach the South a lesson and a lesson half-taught wasn't learned. They had to do it all the way. The soldiers were not about to stop. After weeks of almost total freedom, they would shortly be restrained, and if this was to be their last, they were going to make the most of it. They yanked at women, dragging them off the street. The noise was deafening, shouts, screams, occasional shots, people running, soldiers milling, a few fires breaking out.

He finally couldn't stand it anymore, reasoning that the men who'd killed his family would be in the thick of it. So sick of the spectacle that he couldn't bring himself to look for them, not even sure that he could recognize them, uncertain where the men he'd come with were, he retreated from the city, circling the outskirts, ending up at Sherman's base of operations.

It was to the north, on a plain in full sight of the river and the ocean. Tents were pitched, corrals established, sentries posted. December 21, cold even in Georgia, campfires started, thin gray smoke streams drifting skyward. And even on the plain the commotion from the city was too much for him, the shouts, the screams, the isolated shots, the sound of doors and windows breaking. Fires sent great black clouds that hung and spread and capped the city.

It was just as well that he'd left. He realized now how out of place he must look with his ragged farm clothes, Union cap, and dirty face. Pathetic even. And he knew that he would need some help, some clothes, some food, a place to sleep, and if he'd lost the troopers who had helped him, he would have to find some others. He approached a sentry.

"What is it, boy?"

"I need some food."

"Go away."

"I need some food."

The sentry moved to swat at him, and a soldier walking by reached out to stop him. "What's the trouble?"

"Nothing, sir. This kid here won't go way. I thought I'd make him."

"What's the trouble?" This time to the boy.

"I need some food."

The soldier pursed his lips and told the sentry, "Let him pass." The sentry shrugged. The soldier held out his arm.

The soldier was an officer, a man named Ryerson, and that was the start of everything that mattered.

◨◨◨◨◨◨ 50 ◨◨◨◨◨◨

CALENDAR had been with the Army in the Philippines when they introduced the .45. That was in 1911. He'd been out of the Army quite a while by then, close to sixty years old, and they almost hadn't taken him, forcing him to use every bit of influence he could muster, getting in touch with soldiers he had served with who'd become important. Even then they didn't take him readily. "You'd think that after Cuba and the rest, you'd had enough," they told him. But he hadn't, although he found it difficult to explain. It was partly a question of going stale. For sure it had to do with growing old, but not in a way that anyone understood. All his life he'd gone where the battles took him, seeing new places, learning new ways. Indeed the rhythm of his life had matched the pattern of his country's conflicts, and now that it was in another conflict, he felt incomplete, wanting to be where his instincts said he ought to be. His logic failed him; his emotion was convincing. In the end the people he appealed to owed him so much that they let him go, and it turned out that their warnings were correct. The rigors of that kind of fighting really were too much for him. Thrashing through the jungle; monsoons, yellowjack, malaria; even though he'd withstood diseases well in Cuba, they were now too strong for him, and in a short while he was home.

But none of that was the point. He didn't even mention it. The point was, as he sat by the fire, the first good fire since setting out from Columbus, big and warm and hypnotizing, in contrast to the meager dwindling fire that cold night near the village, the point was, he explained to Prentice, holding it and showing him, the .45 semiautomatic. . . . After the U.S. victory over Spain in Cuba, the Philippines had become the province of America. But when the United States went there to take charge, the natives had revolted. Mostly these were Moros, the Spanish word for Moors—Moslems whose religious zeal in fighting was unlike anything, including the American Indian, that the United States had ever come up against. "They'd come running down the main street of their village, waving those big long knives they had, yelling, and you could hit them two, three times with a rifle or a handgun, and don't ask me how but they'd just keep coming. If you weren't fast enough pulling that trigger often enough, they'd be on to you before you knew it, still strength left in them to slit your throat before they crawled on a ways and died. So we needed something else, something that would really stop them at close range, and this was it. When they got hit with one of these, arm, chest, shoulder, it didn't matter, they stayed hit. This just picked them up and slammed them back, and you still had six more shots for any others, reloading just as easy as slipping in another magazine. If you're at home with guns at all and not afraid of the recoil, you know that it's not as hard to hit somebody with this as people say. It was designed by Browning, but his company never got the patent. Colt did. All the same, it's important to remember Browning, to keep in mind that somebody put this thing together for a reason, to do a certain kind of job, and every time you use it to think of it as a tool, a very special tool with a very special purpose, and you use it with the same precision and respect as any other tool. The only trouble is, you get in country like this, lots of sand and wind, it jams, and all the time you're working to free it, somebody's out there trying to kill you. Depend on it alone and you're dead. You need something else, something like this.''

He reached beneath his vest and pulled out his revolver, a Colt .45 western Peacemaker.

"Sure it's a little more awkward, a little less powerful. It only holds six shells. Reloading seems to take all day. But I've had this over thirty years now, I've taken it everywhere, through every kind of weather and terrain you can imagine, and it's never jammed. It was designed by Colt himself. He whittled the first model on an ocean voyage in 1830, and over the years he perfected it until he finally came up with this. At least his company did. That was in

the seventies, and by then Colt himself was dead. It doesn't matter. He was the man responsible. It's just too bad that he didn't live to see the difference that he made. You use it as a backup gun.'' Now the old man was reaching into his saddle bags, bringing out another one and giving it to Prentice. ''Don't let the sergeant see you with it. He knows it isn't regulation and he'll take it. Keep it in your saddle bags, and when things look like trouble, slip it in your belt back here or over on your side. Make sure you wait until you absolutely have to use it. More than once it'll save your life.

''Now I'm sure you know a lot of that. The facts anyway. But it's like with horses, something you would understand. The more you brush a horse down, feed it, talk to it, the more you study it for any place it's hurting, the more you understand its background, the better you can work with it. It's like you've got to know your horse as well as yourself until the two of you are moving both the same. It's that way with a gun. You take it apart, you clean it, hold it, you never take it off. You learn who made it, why he made it, why the thing turned out the way it did. You know that gun as well as yourself, you treat it as an extension of yourself, you live with it until it's second nature. That's the point. That's the start of everything about this, everything about it that's worth knowing.''

51

"JUST for fun, pretend that I'm your enemy. Get off your horse and walk across to me."

It was morning, and the Thirteenth was preparing to move out. They needed rest, but it didn't matter. Pershing had been anxious for the Columbus column to arrive. Having sent out other units days before, he had left a core of men around him, and now that his other forces were together, he planned several spearheads, east and south and west, deeper into Mexico. There were several rumors as to Villa's whereabouts, and he wanted to pursue them.

Prentice was already mounted, turning where his company was assembling, when the old man suddenly appeared before him, standing to his left and saying that.

Prentice wondered what the old man meant.

"Go on," the old man said.

Prentice looked at him a moment longer, shrugged, got off, and turned to him. The old man had his pistol aimed at him.

"You don't know it, but you're dead. That's not the way to do it. Watch."

He put away his gun, went over to the horse, and let it smell his hand before he drew the hand along its face and neck and gripped the pommel, mounting one-armed, stirrup creaking, stiffly.

112

"Don't dismount in open sight of anybody you don't trust."

"Including you?"

"Including everybody. Remember this with people that you know and you won't forget it with a stranger."

As he spoke, the old man turned the horse so Prentice watched him from the side. Then one-armed, dismounting so only his head and legs showed, nothing else, he came from around the horse, his pistol aimed at him again.

52

PRENTICE thought about it as he rode.

The camp had packed up, splitting into smaller columns, spread out like the fingers of a hand. Pershing's Dodge was at the center, followed by his own troop and the correspondents in their Hudsons and their Fords. At the start the fingers stayed together. Then they split up, heading off toward different lower sections of the compass.

Up ahead, squinting through the dust and haze, Prentice saw the old man riding near the front and recalled what the old man had told him.

"All that sort of thing I can show you, the little tricks and gimmicks, but they don't mean a thing if you don't make them yours, if you don't come up yourself with others like them, only better. Because the point isn't the tricks, it's the attitude behind them, the habit of mind. You can't ever let yourself get careless. You can't ever walk into something, I don't care how innocent or apparently harmless, without figuring on the worst and planning what to do.''

◻◻◻◻◻ 53 ◻◻◻◻◻

"LIKE that snake," the old man said.

They were at a water hole, not much of one, just a pool among some rocks, but they had seen a lizard drinking from it and the pool was clear, so the troop had stopped and group by group had gone to fill canteens and let their horses drink.

Prentice looked. It was a rattler, eight feet from him, motionless beneath a shelf of rock.

"I noticed it the first few seconds we got over here," the old man said, "waiting for you to react. You can't depend on warning. You've got to keep pinching yourself to check around you all the time."

Prentice stepped back from the pool and drew his gun.

"Why?" the old man asked. "He hasn't bothered you. Anyway if Villa is around here and he hasn't seen our dust, he'll surely hear the shot. Think. Don't do anything without first figuring the implications."

Prentice looked at him and, feeling foolish, dropped his aim.

ACTUALLY Villa wasn't anywhere around. His real name was Doroteo Arango. He'd been born in 1878 in the state of Durango, south of Chihuahua, but throughout his career he had spent so much time in and around Chihuahua that he knew it as well as his home state. Considering the lead he had, the expedition would have had trouble tracking him on neutral territory, let alone what amounted to his home. Then too, for close to twenty years he'd had almost constant practice hiding out.

In 1895 he'd been working with his widowed mother, his brothers, and his sisters on a large wealthy Mexican estate. He'd formed a friendship with a local band of cattle thieves, had been implicated in a robbery, had spent several months in prison before a friendly landowner intervened to arrange for his release. Shortly after, his sister having been assaulted, Villa had killed the man responsible, the son of the family on whose estate he worked, and, understanding the first principle of justice at that time—that the rich were always in the right—he had immediately taken to the hills. That was when he was seventeen.

Perhaps to save his family from reprisals, he had changed his name to Francisco Villa, usually known as Pancho, a common nickname for Francisco. Remembering his friendship with the outlaw gang, he had stolen a horse from a rail outside a barroom and had taken up with thieves who operated in Durango and Chihuahua. He may have worked for a time as a field hand in New Mexico, Arizona, and California. There is a rumor that he signed on with Teddy Roosevelt's Rough Riders. For the most part, though, he stayed a bandit, earning a reputation as a kind of Robin Hood, stealing cattle from the great estates, keeping some for himself, selling others, distributing the remainder to poor villages. After all, the reason he was a bandit in the first place was his rebellion against the Mexican aristocrats, and he seems to have taken pleasure in supporting himself at their expense, in helping to reduce the difference between rich and poor.

Those were the Díaz years, thirty years of dictatorship, and when in 1910 the revolution came along, Villa saw a chance to turn from bandit to guerrilla, doing what he'd been doing all along but now for a righteous purpose. He was leader of his own band then, from all accounts a charismatic figure, sometimes with a mustache, sometimes without, not tall, solid though, round-faced, dark-eyed, riveting. One contemporary describes "this big athlete standing up to speak, his huge chest bulging beneath a soft silk shirt, opening to expose his wide bull neck." He had wives all through Mexico, inspired friendship everywhere he went, captivated people by the way he sat a horse, indeed by the very horses that he chose, the biggest, strongest, most impressive he could find.

Considering his talents, then, it is not surprising that once he committed himself to the revolution he quickly turned his band of fifteen men into almost forty thousand. His experience in planning robberies, executing them, and getting away lent itself naturally to guerrilla tactics. In-

deed, his favorite military ploy, the surprise of a sudden night attack, was itself an outcome of his bandit days, and if it had not been for a final disinclination to take charge, he could have been the leader of his country. As it was, he missed his chance. Carranza beat him to it. Thereafter, treated as an outcast, chipped away by Carranza forces, he started losing battles, found the United States turned against him, lost access to supplies, saw his force of forty thousand dwindle to four hundred, and by 1916 his anger at the United States and his need for food and bullets, horses and supplies, had led him to Columbus.

Following the raid, his band reduced to only two hundred, he headed due south as the United States had supposed, but instead of hitting Colonia Dublán and the American Mormons settled there, which the Punitive Expedition was in part intended to prevent, he skirted the place, heading deeper into Mexico toward the mountains farther south.

He stopped at the foothills in a town, El Valle, where he took recruits. The "took" was literal. Some men of the village willingly went with him. Others Villa harangued from the back of a wagon, his men on horseback flanking him while he paced and gestured, his black eyes flashing, and the village men looked down or blank-faced at him, a few just shaking their heads. One young man among them later wrote about it, noting how when they refused he stood them in a line, dismissed the old men, and while the women and children wailed, he ordered his men to take the rest of them with him, under guard.

From El Valle, he pushed farther south to Namiquipa, where he fought and won a battle against Carranza forces. That was on March 18, the same day Pershing's column

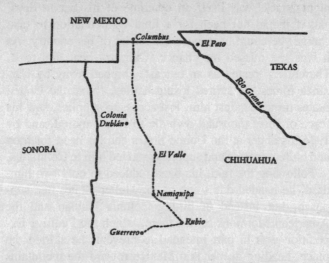

arrived at Colonia Dublán, seventy miles to the north. With a few exceptions Villa would keep that kind of lead, always several days ahead, U.S. forces riding into towns to hear that Villa, having been there, was long gone.

From Namiquipa he headed farther south to Rubio, regrouping to attack Carranza forces at Guerrero, to the west. The attack went well. Indeed, advancing at night, the garrison asleep, no sentries posted, Villa took the place without a shot. The case was otherwise with a garrison in the nearby village of San Isidro. Anticipating resistance, wanting to protect his flank, Villa had sent part of his band to take that troop as well, and there his men encountered such resistance that they were forced to flee, retreating to

Guerrero where pursuing Carranzistas joined them in a major fight.

It made the difference. Actually Villa had already, unknown to himself, made the difference when he took those men from their wives and children at El Valle. Forced now to use every man he had, he'd armed them for the fight, and while he ran ahead to lead the charge, they opened fire, hitting him. Evidently they thought that in the confusion of the fight no one would know which side had shot him. The trouble was that, just when they began to shoot, the other forces had pulled back, leaving no doubt where the bullet came from. The position of the wound—through the leg, from back to front—didn't hide much either. Villa's soldiers swung on them, many peasants dropping rifles, raising arms and shaking heads, jabbering that they didn't know how it had happened. They came that close to being shot.

What saved them was his pain. He was writhing on the ground, his leg bleeding badly, and his men soon gathered around to help him. As much as anyone could tell, he'd been hit by a Remington .44, a very large caliber that left a finger-size hole going in and a fist-size hole going out, traversing the leg from the back of the knee to the shinbone, shattering the shinbone so that for days afterward his men were picking fragments of bone from the wound. They dressed the wound and packed it with splints, set him in a wagon, and, under armed guard, hurried him toward safety. That was shortly after midnight on March 29. All told, 150 men went with him. The rest, what amounted to 100, stayed behind to secure the town and rest. Eight hours later, having been informed that Villa might be at

Guerrero, the Seventh Cavalry, riding through the night to get there, mustered an attack and took the place, killing 56 and wounding 35. If it hadn't been for Villa's recruiting techniques at El Valle and the subsequent revenge the conscripted peasants took on him, the U.S. expedition into Mexico might have ended at Guerrero two weeks after it had started instead of what eventually stretched out to a year.

▣▣▣▣▣ 55 ▣▣▣▣▣

THE wagon rattled toward the summit, jouncing over rocks and fissures, wrenching shrieks from him. The man who drove the wagon squinted through the icy wind and streaking specks of snow that struck him toward the group of men on foot ahead who did their best to clear the route and find the gentlest way. The air was gray, the sky so dark that someone waking might have thought that it was dusk, although it was only afternoon.

To the driver's right a wall of rock rose several hundred feet. To his left the ground gave way forever. Villa shrieked again. The driver looked behind and saw him writhing from the cold and pain, wrapped in blankets, pale and moaning.

The driver looked ahead and saw the roadway narrow. When the wagon came within three feet on either side, an officer rode up and ordered him to stop. The driver pulled back on the reins and set the brake, calling to the men on foot ahead to calm the horses, looking back to where the officer was off his horse and climbing onto the wagon, ordering some men on foot behind to bring a litter they'd prepared, lifting Villa on his own and easing him down toward them.

One man slipped, and Villa tumbled, moaning. Others scrambled for him, shouting, falling. Villa's blankets came unwrapped, showing where his pantleg was slit to the hip, his wound packed by four thick splints, then wrapped with strips of cloth now widely stained with dark, foul-looking blood. His swollen foot was black, not from blood on it but from underneath the skin, from the condition of the foot itself.

Villa shrieked. The officer shouted. The men on foot yelled directions at one another as they fumbled to support Villa, jolting his bad leg, wrapping blankets around him, turning their faces from the odor of the wound. They set him on a litter. Eight men stood on each side, lifting, putting it on top of their shoulders while the officer looked at the driver, telling him to get the wagon going again, and in the snow and wind the procession started forward.

The roadway narrowed even more. At ten thousand feet, the horses rasping loudly, the driver wiped his nose and found that he was bleeding from the altitude. The roadway turned and angled higher. The left rear wheel slipped over. The wagon started shifting as the driver struggled with the reins to stop the horses, but the wagon upended, the driver jumping, landing hard as the wagon flipped and disappeared, the wooden bar that held the horses snapping, and the horses bolted forward, scattering the guides on foot ahead of them. Chaos. The men supporting Villa's litter dropped him.

56

PRENTICE heard the scream and turning saw a trooper scrambling from a gully, his pants down, screaming. He was clutching his arm, running, stumbling toward a group of troopers, but no sooner was he near them than he started running toward another, then another. His eyes were wide, his face pale. He kept screaming.

No one moved. They just stood, staring at him as he ran and screamed. It was almost noon. They'd stopped to walk their horses, then to rest and give them grain and water. The man had evidently gone down to the gully to relieve his bowels, and now it was registering on everybody what must have happened down there, people starting toward him as he swung in circles and clutched his arm and screamed.

"What is it? What's the matter?" Calendar was suddenly among them, grabbing the man.

"The damn thing stung me!"

"What thing? Tell me what it is."

"I'm going to die!"

The man wrenched free, running again, and Calendar stretched out his leg to trip him. The man fell sprawling in the dirt, his buttocks showing, his privates open to the air.

"I asked you what thing. Tell me what it is."

"A scorpion!"

"What kind?"

The man was writhing, his face contorted by pain. "What difference does it make? I'm going to—"

"Let me see your arm."

The man was clutching it, and Calendar reached down to pull the man's hand away.

Prentice stood beside him, looking down. From wrist to elbow, the arm was swollen twice its size, the center of it, on the top, an angry, flaming red.

Prentice shivered. Several troopers gasped.

"It's fine. You're going to be all right," Calendar said.

"I'm going to die." The man grimaced.

"No. You're not. You'll be damn sick for sure, but not enough to kill you. You got lucky. What'd you do? Go down to take a crap? You leaned back without looking, and the next thing you were stung?"

The man thrashed on the ground, nodding fiercely, moaning.

"Well, you could have been stung on your *cojones*. Then you *would* have been in trouble. Or on the side of your arm where the vein is. The main thing is the sting swelled up."

The man writhed, his face contorted, moaning.

"There's two kinds of scorpions. One's a little straw-colored, streamlined job. It spreads its poison through your body, and it kills you. The second's a bigger, wider kind, almost brown. The poison's local. The sting swells up. You've got the second. If your arm was numb instead of burning, if it wasn't swollen, then I'd say to worry. Someone get my saddle bags.''

The man kept moaning all the time Calendar spoke, but Calendar kept talking just the same. It was like he wasn't explaining to him anyhow. He turned to Prentice, looking at him.

Prentice nodded and went for the saddle bags.

57

"WHAT'D you give him?''

"Morphine for the pain. Seconal to slow him down and stop convulsions.''

They were standing close together with their horses, tightening their saddle girths, preparing to mount. The old man strained to pull the strap taut while he fastened it, but one-armed he was clumsy and he finally asked the boy to help him.

"The tourniquet I had you fix was obvious enough,'' Calendar said and watched the boy as he finished with the strap and dropped the stirrup from the saddle. "The poison's local, sure, but there's no point in allowing it to spread any farther than it has to. If we were near a town, we might have been able to get some ice and pack the sting to keep the swelling down. Those wet bandages I had you wrap around it serve the purpose, but really ice is better.''

Calendar stood by the horse's head, holding the reins, looking at Prentice.

"The facts I take for granted," Calendar said. "You saw what happened. You shouldn't ever get stung that way yourself now, and you shouldn't wonder what to do if someone else gets stung. You ought to have a first-aid kit like mine that you carry in your saddle bags—potassium permanganate, morphine, that sort of thing—and you ought to know a hundred other things just like this. It's like you shouldn't ever go up against somebody unless you know him as well as yourself, know all there is about him. That's the way it is with everything. You've only got one business, and that's to be an expert. If you want to learn about all this, you just keep watching and remember.

"But there's something else, something that I *don't* take for granted, not the facts but how to react to them. This matter I keep mentioning of attitude. It's like that fool charging up out of the gully, wasting energy, running around, screaming. The sting wasn't going to kill him, but the shock and panic might have. I knew a fellow once, walking through some foothills in Wyoming. Stepped over a log, looked down at where his boot was in the circle of a rattler, dropped dead on the spot. Turned out the snake wasn't even alive, but this fellow let his emotions get the better of him. You've got to keep control. So you're stung by a scorpion, so what do you do, run around screaming, or do you try to figure what to do about it? That's the key. There'll be all kinds of things that happen to you that you can't control, but once they do, you can control how you respond to them. You never do anything without a reason. You learn the facts, and then you figure what to do about them. The first isn't any good without the second. Learn just the first, and you'll be dead.''

All the time the old man talked, the column had been grouping. The sergeant had been riding up and down, telling them to mount. The old man had been holding up his hand to tell the boy to wait until he was finished. Now the old man stopped and looked at him, and, almost as if the speech had been mechanical, something apart from him that nonetheless needed to be finished, Calendar paused, abruptly turned, and with his good arm gripped the saddle horn, put his boot in the stirrup, and mounted. Calendar studied Prentice, told him, ''Thanks for helping with the saddle,'' then nudged his horse and rode off toward the front.

Prentice watched him go. He took a moment before he realized that he was the only trooper who wasn't mounted with the column. They were all over there on horseback, watching him, and he slid up onto the saddle, riding over.

''I'll be damned,'' the sergeant told him, waiting for him. ''I never saw him talk that long to anyone.''

58

THEY'D come up through a break between two cliffs that years later Calendar would think of when the Columbus column, pursued by Mexican federals, pushed through a break just like it and worked across that sandy basin.

Indeed, as Calendar came charging from the break, cavalry spreading out in panic all around him, bullets sounding, he'd almost expected to see a river down there, a fertile valley spreading out before him, an island in the middle of the river. But of course there hadn't been a river, or any fertile valley, just that sandy basin that they'd worked across, and while just for a moment Calendar had that sense of having been there once before, that it was all going to happen just like then, the feeling passed as quickly as it had come and the action turned out very different. But then that had been in another time and country. The river was the Arikaree in what we now call eastern Colorado. The strip of land in the middle of the river would soon be known as Beecher's Island. The year was 1868.

There were fifty of them. They'd been ten days out from home base at Fort Wallace, Kansas, traveling light on forced march, trailing Indians. The Indians, mostly Sioux and Cheyenne, some Arapaho, had seen enough land taken from them by the whites and now had struck back, hitting wagon trains and settlements, stage stations, ranches, any place they came across. Then, striking fast and running, they had split up into smaller groups, then smaller yet, fanning out across the plains until chasing them was futile. It was the kind of action that an army three years from the Civil War was unaccustomed to. Trained to fight large battles using complex tactics, troops would wait at forts until word came of a raid, then mount a major expedition, bogged down by equipment and supply lines, moving so slowly that they had no hope of catching anyone.

These troops were part of what the Army called its Division of the Missouri, supervised by Sheridan, who himself was supervised by Sherman. Both had been Union generals in the Civil War and their names were synonymous with terrorism, Sheridan in the Shenandoah Valley of Virginia, Sherman in the southeast route through Georgia. Even so, they took a while before they thought of using similar terrorist tactics against the Indians. As the Indian raids grew worse and conventional tactics clearly became unworkable, Sheridan and Sherman finally made their choice, deciding not to wait until the Indians struck again but rather to go out and strike the Indians, sending out small groups of fifty lightly armed, fast-traveling men whose object was to track down Indians and force them to a fight. On this day, September 16, 1868, just such a group was engaged in that objective.

They'd been spotting signs for several days now, here and there at first, occasional tracks or droppings or extinguished fires, then more of them and wider, fresher, clearer, other groups of tracks coming from each side and merging with the first. By afternoon of this day, they didn't even need to look to follow. Ahead of them the grassland was packed down and trampled from left to right two hundred yards across. It looked, one scout informed them, like the path of several villages.

The man in charge was Major George A. Forsyth. Under Sheridan he had been a brevet brigadier general in the Union army, and after the Civil War had been demoted to a major, as the Army cut back and regrouped. He understood that unless he stood out in his job he'd never have another chance for better rank and pushed his men accordingly. Bothered by the evident number of Indians ahead of them, one scout had suggested they turn back. "Enlisted to fight Indians, didn't you?" Forsyth had snapped back and ordered the column farther on. All the same, he wasn't foolish or proud in the manner of Custer. He knew his job and took precautions, sending points ahead to check the draw as they moved forward, the troopers feeling nervous as they reached it, riding through and coming out the other side. The valley stretched off quite a way, the trail they followed leading straight across. Forsyth waited while his scouts reported. Then, squinting toward the setting sun, he made his choice, led the column toward the river, and they camped.

Calendar had always thought it ironic that the man responsible for his being with that column was the man who was then his ultimate superior, General Sherman. Following Savannah, he had stayed with Sherman's army, not so much to find the men who'd killed his family, although he still had hopes of that, but out of simple common sense. The South was going to lose. There was no doubt of that. What Sherman had done in Georgia, and Sheridan in Virginia, made it clear that if the South kept fighting, the North wouldn't just defeat it but destroy it, scour it from the earth. Already the Confederacy had been reduced to Virginia and the Carolinas. Sherman was marching toward the Carolinas. Grant and Sheridan were flanking Lee in Virginia. The last place a southern boy would want to be was on his own or with the southern army, especially one like himself whose loyalty had been to his home and family, not the state or the idea of the South. Calendar's family hadn't owned slaves anyhow, and if the victors had left him and his family to themselves, it wouldn't have mattered to him who had won.

He opted for the North, playing now the role of helpless orphan, appealing to a sense of guilt yet leaving vague the circumstances of his family's death lest someone come to fear they couldn't trust him. Mostly he just kept his eyes on Captain Ryerson, the officer who'd befriended him. Calendar stayed close to him, going with him everywhere he could, partly because no one else had expressed the same degree of sympathy toward him, partly because he'd explained how all alone he was and made what he thought was an equitable proposition. If the officer would look after him, he in turn would look after the officer, seeing to his needs, polishing his equipment, running errands, serving as a kind of orderly. Depending on the point of view, it was a relation of convenience or necessity, and it worked. In time they grew accustomed to each other. The captain worked with him to mute his Georgia accent, gave him books to read, taught him different ways to speak—the phrase *equitable proposition*, for example, wasn't Calendar's but Ryerson's, but the boy soon made it, along with many others like it, his. (This was the source of what years later was the peculiar blend of slang and proper speech that Calendar would use with Prentice.) The boy was eager to impress, and the officer responded. By the start of spring, Calendar's position was secure. What was more, he acted and talked like he was from the North. Soldiers forgot the reason Calendar had come to be with them. They seemed to feel secure around him.

Finally, on April 9, Palm Sunday, Lee surrendered. The war was over. The army stayed intact for several months, then started breaking up. "We're going home," the soldiers said. The only trouble was that the boy had no home to go back to. He thought of going back to claim his family's land, but he didn't see how he could till it, let alone hang on to it. Already rumors had begun about Union tax collectors, about northern speculators coming down to take what land they could. Plus, whether the war was over or not, Calendar knew what reaction he could expect from Georgia families who had lived through Sherman's march and now discovered he had taken up with Sherman's men. He could try to hide where he had been the past half-year, but he knew one way or another they'd find out. Just turned fourteen, in his position, he didn't see what he could do.

He kept his eyes on Ryerson as each day the captain prepared to muster out, making arrangements, going through the paperwork, seeing off his men. Then the troop was fairly well disbanded. Those who stayed were reassigned to other units. There wasn't much that remained to do. One day Ryerson came from his tent, and he was out of uniform. He wore a red-plaid shirt and a pair of pants from before he'd joined the war. He was wearing his officer's holster and revolver, his officer's boots, a work hat, and suspenders. A pair of saddle bags was slung across his shoulder. He was carrying his saber and his rifle. He nodded to the boy, who hollow-stomached followed as Ryerson walked over to the horse that he had earlier told the boy to saddle for him. The boy stood by him as Ryerson got up on the horse and looked at him.

"So where will you go?" Ryerson asked, easing the rifle into its scabbard, pushing the saber down beside it.

"I'm not sure." Calendar shrugged, determined not to let Ryerson know he was disappointed to see him go.

"Why not come with me?" Ryerson said it so offhandedly that the boy wasn't even sure he'd heard right. Then his heart skipped and his stomach started burning and he did his best to keep control. He shrugged again and asked, "Where'd you have in mind?"

"I'm not sure myself. West maybe. One thing's sure. There's not a whole lot here."

"Thought you had family in New York."

"That's right, I do." Ryerson looked at him, rocking slowly in the saddle. "But I guess they'll have to do without me. It's not a wife or anything, just a sister and her children. She lost her husband in the war. I was considering going back and helping her, but it's like I've been doing so much for everybody else, it's about time I did something for myself. So what do you say?"

"I'm thinking on it."

"Well, don't think too long, or I just might up and leave you."

"How far west exactly?"

"Ever see the Mississippi?"

Calendar shook his head.

"Well, I think we'll go a lot beyond that. I think we'll see some land. What's the matter?"

"How come it took you so long to ask me?"

"I wasn't sure I wanted you along. Now I am."

Calendar thought about it. "I'd need a horse."

"I'll get you one."

"I'd need another set of clothes, a rifle maybe."

"I'll get them."

"Why?"

"If I knew that, I'd know why I took so long to ask you in the first place. Are you coming or not?"

"I'm coming."

"All right then." Ryerson reached down his open hand.

The boy didn't know what he was doing. Then he realized, shaking hands with him. His heart was racing even faster, although he did his best not to show it. All the same, he found that he was smiling, a big wide grin that stretched his cheeks and set his eyes to aching. Ryerson smiled back. The boy tried, but he couldn't see him clearly, eyes dim, cheeks wet, tasting salty. He couldn't breathe. His throat felt swollen. For the first time since his family had been murdered, Calendar cried, smiling badly, gently weeping.

And they did see land, a lot of it, heading northwest from the Carolinas through Tennessee and Kentucky toward Missouri and St. Louis. At first along the way they saw charred farms and trampled fields, soldiers now in work clothes walking along the roads. Sometimes North and South would meet and break out into hand fights. Mostly they just stared and cursed and, standing straighter, walked on by.

Calendar and Ryerson stayed away from towns, camping hidden in the woods, shooting game, working as field hands in exchange for food and clothes. No one had much money. The farther they got, the less stark things appeared, drifters smiling now and then, farmers taking time to talk with them, people going on about their lives. Even so, they never felt that they were out of it until they reached St. Louis. An important Union depot in the war, it had gone untouched, prospering, serving as a gateway to the West, buildings going up, people swarming in. They got there in late fall, the weather turning cold; stayed there for the winter, working on construction; left in early spring, signing on as hunters for a wagon train. And they were good at it. That was one thing Calendar knew, that and horses—hunting buffalo and prairie jack, deer and anything else they came across, even though the meat was mostly out of season. It took them all the way to Colorado. From there they left the wagon train and traveled north, working for a year as trail hands in Wyoming. Then they signed on with the cavalry. It seemed an easy thing to do. Ryerson helped Calendar lie about his age. Sixteen now, he looked like twenty. They didn't have much trouble.

Now they stood where the troop had camped in that eastern Colorado valley, looking past the river toward the long rich grass and far-off sloping hills. The sun was setting to their left, casting everything in alpenglow. They looked down at the river. The bed was wide—as much as they could tell, two hundred yards across. This time of year the water wasn't much though, occupying only half of the channel, sand on each side, splitting in the middle to go around an island that was short and narrow, thick with scrubbrush, cottonwood, and willow. The soldiers turned and looked behind them toward the other line of hills and the break that they had come through. They spread their arms and breathed the cool clean air. They caught each other's eyes and didn't need to say it. There was something wrong about the place.

They'd learned about that fairly early: There were certain places where you knew you shouldn't stay. There wouldn't be a reason for the feeling, no bad aspect to a place, no rumors about it, just a vague uneasy feeling that they shouldn't stay. Pressed to understand it, they had talked about the way poles of two magnets could repel each other. Some spots felt like home and others didn't, and when you reached a spot that didn't, you moved on. They knew that most times they were being overcareful, but out here being overcareful was a virtue, and they always followed through on it.

Now they felt the same. There wasn't anything about the place they didn't like. Indeed, in one sense it was lovely. Granted it was in the open, but they had camped

out in the open many times. Granted too that they were camped near Indians, but they had camped near Indians before as well, and there wasn't any sign now that the Indians had spotted them. Anyhow, where else was there to go? The horses needed water. There hadn't been a good place in the hills. This was the best they could find. Maybe that was it. The place was too good: Indians passing by would know that anyone on their trail would pick this site for a camp. There wasn't anything they could do about it anyhow. The major had made his choice. The sun was almost gone. No place to go. They'd made their spot, and now they would have to stay.

All the same, they checked their weapons, leaving their rifles beside them where they spread their blankets in a hollow in the camp. For his part, Major Forsyth refused permission to light fires, posted extra sentries, and staked the horses near where the men lay. It wasn't so much that he was nervous, just that he was being careful. Even so, several troopers did seem nervous. Calendar was watching them as he set down his saddle and his blanket. They were checking their rifles and their handguns just the way that he and Ryerson had done, working the actions, making sure that they were fully loaded, setting them beside them. Few men were talking. Those who were got short distracted statements in reply. The ones who'd been out here the longest seemed the most preoccupied. Calendar looked and saw that Ryerson was staring at him, and again they didn't need to speak. If more than just the two of them were feeling it, something certainly was wrong. They stretched beneath their blankets, hands on rifles, waited, stood their watch, waited even more, drowsed, and the first wave hit them shortly after dawn.

The whooping was enough to wake them. They lay blinking for a moment. Then they heard the shots and scrambled from their blankets, grabbing rifles, running toward the shots. There were eight Indians, riding down a slight rise to the west, heading toward the horses. Sentries opened up on them. One rider dropped. Another clutched his arm and kept on coming. Calendar and Ryerson opened up as well, others joining in. Another rider dropped, the six survivors swinging to the left and heading back.

"Mount up!" the major ordered. "Dammit, let's get out of here!"

Because in back of those six Indians, up on top the slight rise they were heading back to, left to right on both sides of the river, a line of Indians was spread out that were more than anyone had time to count. Six troopers stood guard, rifles ready, as a backup. The rest were running, grabbing saddles, rushing to their horses, putting on the saddles, cinching them, reaching for their bridles. The troopers who had stayed behind were running toward their saddles now as well. Calendar had thought how stupidly those Indians had come down trying for the horses, warning them. If that was how they fought, a troop as organized as this would have no trouble handling them. He blurted that to Ryerson, trying to maintain himself, and Ryerson quickly set him straight. It wasn't stupid. They were confident, so sure they would win that they had given up surprise to let their youngest braves come boldly down to show their skill.

By then the second wave had started toward them, a third wave close behind. The six remaining troopers were saddled now, the others glancing nervously behind them while the major gave the order to move out, and some were going even as he said it, kicking at their horses, flailing them to hurry as the others broke out into a gallop, riding, cursing, shots and whoops behind them, toward the southeast and the nearby line of hills. Up until then, even in the war, Calendar could not remember being scared like this. Everything was blurred, his reactions automatic. All he thought was what the major obviously was thinking. Get to the high ground. Get to the draw that they had come through. Once they got up in there and controlled it, they could hold back anyone who came through after them.

It was obvious all right. Too much so. The major was suddenly swinging to the left, veering from the hills, leading them in an arc that went the way that they had come. The fleeing troopers started slowing in confusion. They looked at the open draw, then at the Indians charging behind them. The major shouted, waving toward the river, riding back to it. The troopers, caught between their need to get away and their habit of obedience, milled and followed, and that's what saved them. Later it turned out that the Indians wanted them to ride up through the draw. They had others hidden there, prepared to trap the troopers in a cross fire. Forsyth had suspected this, but he wasn't sure, forced to make a quick decision, returning to their camp, and if it hadn't been for the luck of his followers' instincts, the column would have been wiped out. As it was, they thought he had seen what they themselves had not, returning with him before they realized the full significance of what was going on. By the time they understood that there was no clear reason why they should not ride up through the draw, it was too late. They were so far toward the river that they had no choice. They had to keep on going toward the river or stay out in the open and be shot.

Their fear then changed to rage, and they cursed at him, shouting as they followed him across the river to the scrubbrush island, leaping from their horses, tying them, still cursing as they pulled out rifles, bracing for the charge. One trooper still was undecided, milling with his horse, shouting, "Don't let's stay here! We'll be killed!" starting toward the draw, the major grabbing at his arm and pointing with his handgun, telling him, "You move, I'll blow your head off!" whirling then and firing toward the charge.

The first bullet from out there dropped the trooper from his horse. The other soldiers, rifles out, had tied their horses in a circle, in a kind of barricade, diving down to shoot between their horses' hooves, staying far enough away to keep from being trampled by them. The soldiers were pushing dirt before them, squeezing off their shots, going back to digging, squirming, firing again. The major was still standing, giving them directions as, the first wave just about to hit them, a soldier pulled him down. The Indians came, what looked to be at least a hundred of them, off the bank across the sand and through the water, charging toward the soldiers, shooting, screaming, riding bareback, naked but for strips of cloth around their waists and privates, some with feathered bonnets, all with faces splashed with red and green, eyes wide, faces twisted, shooting, screaming, and the troopers, caught up in their frenzy, really opened up, firing as quickly as they could work their rifles, emptying them, switching to their handguns, emptying them as well, scrambling to reload. These last were six-shot Colt revolvers, cruder than the later famous western versions, nonetheless effective. The rifles were repeating Spencers, lever actions, six rounds in the magazine and one more in the chamber. Thirteen shots per man, almost fifty men; in less than thirty seconds they pumped all those bullets at the first wave coming toward them, dropping almost half and breaking up the charge.

The powder in their cartridges was black instead of later smokeless. The thick gray cloud that gathered screened the Indians as they veered to either side, following the way the river split around the island. The troopers, ramming bullets into their rifles, strained to see and fired with them, dropping more, fumbling to keep loading. In the smoke the Indians galloped up the other bank, swung to regroup, charged back, and this time they were easier to split, parting around the island again, rifles sounding, mouths wide, screaming, galloping up the bank that they had first come down.

The troopers barely had a chance to breathe, making sure that they'd reloaded, when the other wave was close upon them. This time, though, the soldiers broke the charge before it reached the river, firing now so surely and quickly, smoke cloud forming, that the Indians with another hundred yards to go were already swinging to the left and working back the way they'd come.

Then, as fast as it had started, smoke cloud rising, it was over. Some troopers kept on firing, but the major didn't need to tell them to ease up—it was obvious that they had to. They would need every round they had. As it was, they hadn't much. One hundred and forty rounds on each man for the rifles, thirty for the handguns, an additional four thousand on a pack mule for the rifles. They'd each used up nearly thirty rounds on these two charges, and from now on they would have to save their shots until they were sure.

Easy to say. Or think, at any rate. No one talked about

it. The piles of empty cartridges around them made it clear. The smoke was almost gone. The few who had continued shooting quickly stopped. The rest, the pressure of battle off them for a moment, were working hard to reload. For sure, the Indians showed no sign of leaving. The main group was still spread out on the rise across from them. Calendar stared through the space between his horse's hooves. He was a careful distance from the hooves, near a clump of trampled scrubbrush, a mound of freshly dug dirt before him, reloading as the others were, breathing quickly, staring toward the Indians. They were small and indistinct out there, sitting on their horses, calmly waiting.

The silence was a shock to him. All he heard was the harsh sound of his breathing, and even that was strange, as if it didn't come from outside through his mouth and nostrils but from inside through his chest and throat, somewhere in his head. It came to him muffled. Then he registered the ringing in his head as well, in both ears, a high-pitched constant *ting*, louder than his breathing, louder than anything. He'd never been among such heavy shooting, all around him, blasting near both ears, unable to distinguish his own shots from all the others. Sometimes, as a boy, hunting in thick woods in Georgia, he had shot and set one ear ringing slightly but not enough to bother him, and if there had been time and he knew he wouldn't spook his quarry, he had blocked that ear with bits of cloth. But now there hadn't been a chance for that, and he wouldn't have thought to do it anyhow, so unfamiliar was this to him.

He shook his head to clear it, but he couldn't stop the ringing, in a panic now, knowing there were sounds around him, people talking, moving, but he couldn't hear them.

Weren't they having trouble with their ears as well? If they were, they didn't show it. Then he registered that he was wet, on his stomach, on his legs, and his first thought was that he'd been hit, and he groped frantically, realizing that in his fright he'd lost control of his bladder, feeling quickly behind him but at least he had control of his bowels. A few others hadn't. The smell was unmistakable. There wasn't anything wrong with his sense of smell, anyhow. He looked around, and nobody seemed to notice, or if they did, they didn't seem to care. There didn't seem any disgrace to it. They were digging themselves deeper into the ground, pushing dirt around them, using knives, metal plates, anything that they could find. Ryerson was one man over to his left, digging fast. Calendar did the same, suddenly realizing that for a little time now he'd been hearing the scratch of metal against soil, the muffled snort of horses, the hooves ahead of him clomping nervously on the ground. His hearing was coming back, not much but a little, and as he relaxed enough to pay less attention to himself, more to what was going on around him, he understood that there were men around him who weren't moving, others holding tightly to themselves, wincing, horses down, chests heaving, frothing blood. He looked behind and saw five troopers crouched around a sixth and talking to him. They parted, and Calendar saw it was the major: He'd been hit in the shin, his pantleg red on blue. The red was spreading, someone putting on a tourniquet. The major's face was gray.

"Get me over there where I can see," Calendar heard the major groan. The words came muffled through the ringing in his ears.

Calendar saw them drag the major toward him, the

major staring past him through the space beneath the horse's stomach toward the Indians out there. The Indians looked like they were getting ready again, milling with their horses, moving into position, looking behind them, then to one side as though watching something come along the rise behind them. Something showed, the tip of something, then a head, a body, a solitary rider coming up abreast of them, then riding out in front. He seemed to make a difference. The Indians started whooping and then skittered with their horses. What the troopers had first seen was the tip of a headdress, long and wide and flowing, filled with feathers.

"Lordy," someone said.

Calendar turned. It was one scout, the oldest of the four, grizzled, dressed in buckskin, tattered fringes dangling from it.

Wincing from his wound, Major Forsyth turned as well. They were stretched out close together, staring toward the rise.

"What is it?"

"Him." The scout shook his head and spat.

"Well, what about him?"

"The Cheyenne call him Bat. You can't tell from here, but up close he's a sight. Big. You can't imagine. Muscles all across him. Face like on a statue. I know him by that headdress. It's one of a kind. They don't wear all them feathers without earning them."

"I never heard of him."

"Sure you have. You'd call him Roman Nose."

"Dear God."

Even Calendar had heard of him. The Indian was known to whites by his broad hooked nose, which must have been what reminded the scout of a statue. The stories told about him were chilling. Bodies dismembered, disemboweled, mutilated until there wasn't any human semblance left to them. Roman Nose wouldn't give up. Once engaged in a fight, he wouldn't stop until one side or the other was annihilated. So far the losing side had always been the whites.

"Well, Jesus, now we're in for it." The major groaned. He used both hands to move his leg from where his weight was partly on it. "I want three troopers in that long grass up ahead. Up there where the island points." He looked around. "You three get going."

Calendar took a moment before he realized that the major was staring toward him, the man next to him, and Ryerson. They all looked at one another, then back at the major. The man next to him opened his mouth.

"I want you looking at those bodies out there," the major said. "I want you certain they're dead. The next charge, some of them will have been faking. They'll start crawling toward us, and I want them stopped. We'll have enough to worry about dealing with those horsemen." Forsyth waved three other troopers toward the island's other end, then frowned at Calendar. "Well, what are you waiting for?"

Calendar hesitated, looked at Ryerson, looked at the major, grabbed his rifle, and started slowly forward. He squirmed between his horse's front and back legs, reached the grass, and entered. It was prairie grass, tall and brown, topped with rows of seeds. It was dry and brittle, snapping as he crawled. Next to him, the ringing in his ears diminishing, he heard the other man and Ryerson. He felt the beating of his heart against the ground. Then he reached where the grass stopped and the dirt sloped to the river. He could see the Indians face down in the shallow water, others face up beyond the water, in the sand. He crawled back a little, keeping a line of grass in front of him, just enough to see through. The grass smelled like his father's barn.

He shut the thought out, staring toward the fallen Indians. He was moved to speak, to talk to Ryerson, but he knew he shouldn't. If any of them out there were alive, they'd hear the voices and be much more cautious. He looked beyond them toward the line of Indians.

And blinked. They weren't there anymore. They'd already started down. In the brief time he had checked the river, they'd already come that far, and his ears must still have been quite bad because even though the horses were galloping and the Indians had their arms up, waving, faces working, shouting, he couldn't hear them yet. He looked at the biggest Indian, the one the scout called Roman Nose, the one with the huge wide flowing bonnet who was leading them, and the Indian had his rifle raised above his head, shaking it, and the ease with which he did it made the gun seem weightless. Then Calendar thought he saw something move along the riverbank and quickly looked at the bodies there.

Nothing. At least he thought it was nothing. He couldn't be sure. He kept glancing from them to the line of charging Indians, then back to the bodies along the river. His hands were clenched around his rifle.

Some troopers started firing.

"No!" he dimly heard the major shout. "Not until I say! Make sure you're loaded! Fire in volleys!"

The shooting stopped.

Then the Indians started, a few at first, some distance off, then more and more the closer they came.

They came even closer.

One trooper fired.

"Not until I tell you!" the major yelled. "Remember what I said! In volleys!"

The Indians were even closer. Calendar couldn't believe that the major was letting them get this close before he gave the order. He could see the muscles on their stomachs now, as they fired, seventy yards, fifty, horses rumbling.

"Now!" the major said.

And that's what the soldiers had been waiting for, firing, like a cannon going off, one long quick string of blasts on top of one another, deafening, slamming back riders, tumbling horses, taking out the men in front. All except the one who led them.

"Now!" the major yelled again, and again they fired, bodies dropping, horses falling.

And again. And again, riders vaulting fallen bodies, charging, shooting, screaming, Calendar staring out at them, twenty yards away and looming larger, almost onto him, his stomach burning as a painted face appeared before him in the grass.

It was one of the Indians who'd been lying near the river, pretending to be dead, taking advantage of the charge to crawl up on the island. They stared at each other, faces stiff with shock, Calendar recoiling as the major shouted "Now!" and the next thing Calendar had pulled the trigger. The face disintegrated in front of him. Something wet struck him, but he couldn't tell if it was blood or water from the river because the Indians were through it, on the island now, water dripping from the horses surging past him as he swung with them and aimed at one in front, shooting, hitting him almost point blank in the back. The force of the shot dropped horse and rider, whipping them down to the water where the horse regained its footing, running off, and the Indian stayed in the water, face down, floating.

It had happened so fast that Calendar at first didn't even know what he had done, let alone whom he'd shot, but now he saw that it was the one who had led the charge, the one called Roman Nose, and the Indians were slowing, shouting, as the major yelled out, "Now!" again, and the volley shattered them, spilling riders, spooking horses, breaking up the charge. The Indians split, passed the island, and didn't bother to regroup, cutting across the river farther down, heading back the way they'd come.

Reloading quickly, troopers cheered. Horses, gutshot, whimpered. Wounded troopers moaned. There was a sound of metal on metal all through the island, bullets being pushed into magazines, levers working, rifles ready once again, smoke from gunshots drifting. Calendar scanned the fallen riders ahead of him to make sure none of them was going to crawl up into the grass with him. He licked his lips.

"Can they do better?" he heard the major ask, and, turning, he saw the scout beside the major shake his head. Later the scout told them that in all his years he'd never seen a charge to equal it. By all rights the column should be dead. All that had saved them was Roman Nose in the river. If he had still been alive to give the Indians spirit, there wouldn't have been a thing that could have stopped them.

Several troopers claimed their bullet was the one that

had killed him. Calendar never argued it. He knew and didn't see a point in getting into a fight about it. Later, when the soldiers were up and checking the bodies near the river, Calendar went down to Roman Nose and turned him, seeing where his bullet had gone in, directly at the bottom of the spine, ranging up and blasting through the chest. There wasn't any doubt that he was the one who had killed him. He stared at the water rich with blood, looked at the water-soaked headdress, and left it. Another trooper grabbed it. One wounded Indian later told them how their leader hadn't planned to join the fight. His bonnet had some magic to it that prevented him from being struck in battle. But the magic had some taboo that went with it, and the taboo had been violated. For Roman Nose to cleanse himself would have taken quite a while, so he hadn't planned to join the fight, wouldn't have if another chief, jealous of him, hadn't called him womanly.

The way the Indian told it, the story was a long one and a good one, and Calendar had been eager to tell Ryerson, but he never got the chance. Shortly after the charge had broken up, after he had gotten control of himself and felt safe enough not to keep looking out there, he had crawled a little to his left, toward the man next to him and Ryerson, and the man next to him had been stuffing a cloth under Ryerson's shirt where he'd been gutshot. The blood was pouring out. The excitement that Calendar had felt drained from him. He crawled numbly next to Ryerson, cradled him, talked to him, tried to get him to speak, but while Ryerson's eyes flickered and sometimes even seemed to recognize him, he never did say anything, just finally passed out, and against all justice took a day and a night to die. Calendar sat there, cradling him, and cried. That was why he didn't make an issue of who had killed the Indian. He was too full with grief to make room for anger or even pride.

The Indians didn't go away. They didn't charge again, just laid siege. All the troopers' horses were dead. A third of the men were wounded or dead. The next in command, Lieutenant Beecher, was dead as well, and it was for him that the island was named. The major had been hit twice more, a glancing wound against his head and a bullet in his thigh against the artery. He lay like that four days until he knew he'd have to get the bullet out, but the surgeon with them had been killed as well, and everybody else was afraid to do it, fearful that, probing with the knife, they'd strike the artery. Finally the major told two men to hold his leg, and taking his razor from his saddle bags, he worked the bullet out himself. It was the only time during the siege, watching the major do that, nothing for his pain, that Calendar forgot Ryerson. Otherwise he watched everything dully, the way the night after Roman Nose was killed the major had sent two scouts on foot to go for help, how they set out wearing moccasins, walking backward to make their tracks look like Indians stalking toward the island, how two nights later the major had sent the other two, knowing they would move by night and hide by day, how one week later a relief column had come down through the pass and broken the siege, the troopers by then having used up all their rations, roasting putrid horsemeat, the major propped against a tree, resting his leg, reading a book that he had taken with him, *Oliver Twist*. The troopers had cheered when they saw the first men coming through the draw, had stood up, waving shirts and firing rifles. The major had told them to save their bullets. The dead troopers had all been buried by then, the island not large enough for anything but a mass grave, the Indians in and near the river dragged up on the other shore and burned. And Calendar sat near the corner of the mass grave where he had buried Ryerson, holding Ryerson's rifle and his handgun, the man's saddle bags beside him, having already gone through them looking for some name or some address that would tell him how to get in touch with the dead man's sister. But there wasn't any.

59

"GET your ass out of here."

At first Prentice didn't understand. They had stopped for the night, camping at the bottom of a steep, jagged ridge. The site was chosen well, one flank protected, water nearby, brush for making fires. The ridge was to the east. To the west the sun was going down, but with only open ground out there, the light would stay for quite a while.

And the evening started well, everyone in good spirits even after the long hot day's ride, troopers talking as they groomed and fed their horses, tying them, a few men whistling as they spread out bedrolls, others starting fires, sitting down to watch the flames and fry some meat and bread.

When Calendar returned from the ridge, where he had been checking things, he had sat down by a fire and Prentice had joined him. The two had poured coffee and sipped it. The old man had not shaved in several days, his whisker stubble showing rough and gray on his face, aging him, and he'd just set down his cup and rolled a cigarette when he'd spoken, his hand poised with a match against a rock.

Prentice didn't know whom the old man meant. Several troopers who had come to sit down near them wondered too. They looked at one another. Prentice felt his stomach turn, afraid the old man meant himself. Everyone was quiet. He looked at the old man sitting there, his hand poised with the match, his jaw tense, staring toward the fire, and it wasn't just that he didn't know who the old man had in mind—he had never heard him speak that way. Oh, sure, the vulgarity was common enough, and everyone on occasion used it, including the old man. But it was the way he said it, almost like he wasn't human, growling the words, forcing them deep from his throat, twisting them from his voice box.

"Yes, *you*," the old man snarled, his facial muscles working, looking slowly up, staring at the trooper straight across from him. "You know who I'm talking to. I told you get your ass out of here."

The trooper was shifting nervously, hands up. "Listen, really—"

"Hey," the old man said. "I'm talking to you. Don't you hear me talking to you? What the hell's the matter with you?"

It was an Indian, one of the Apaches that the major had signed on to supplement the whites as scouts, and now that Prentice thought about it, he had been aware of someone coming up to stand near them. The Indian was maybe five feet ten, trim and solid, dark-faced with high cheekbones and long hair that hung below his trooper's hat. He wore a mixture of Indian and cavalry clothes, moccasins, regulation khaki pants with a sand-colored hempen shirt hanging at the waist, a webbed gunbelt, semiautomatic pistol in its holster at one side, a yellow bandanna tied around his neck. He stood flat-footed, his pelvis slightly forward, short-legged, long-armed, loose yet tense, his short chin, thin face, and high cheekbones drawing attention to his eyes. He didn't move and he didn't say a word, just kept looking at the old man with those eyes, and they seemed about as deep and dark as eyes could get. It was like there was no bottom to them. "Well, what's it going to be?" the eyes seemed to say. "How far do you want to play?"

The old man threw down his cigarette and match and stood to face the man. "I asked you what the hell's the matter with you. Don't you hear me talking to you? Get away."

The Indian didn't move.

"What are you doing here anyhow? What are you doing sneaking around staring at me?"

The Indian cocked his head and shrugged. He looked to see who else was in on this and, satisfied, glanced back at the old man, staring at him. The old man's face was livid now, contorted, his beard stubble jutting. Prentice had never seen it like this, ugly.

"Well then," the old man said. "I'm not about to tell you anymore." His hand was on his holstered pistol.

And then something happened. *Electric* was the only word that Prentice could later think of. Like touching an exposed wire. The old man said something sharp and quick in a language that Prentice had never heard before but that he assumed was Apache. The Indian didn't move, but everything about the Indian seemed to change, draw in, almost coil. Mostly the change was in his eyes. They seemed to narrow. Not much but enough. And then the Indian answered him, speaking softly and slowly in that language. It was the most beautiful man's voice Prentice had ever heard. The old man spoke to him again, saying almost exactly what he'd said before, except that there was some slight difference in the middle, and the words seemed to take a little longer, and suddenly the Indian was coming for him. His movement was as quick as a rattlesnake's. Prentice had no more than blinked when the Indian was almost on the old man, his knife out where he'd kept it in a sheath at his back, slicing toward the old man's stomach.

And the old man must have been waiting for it. He had to have been, the way he dodged sideways suddenly, stepping back, his good hand out, grabbing the Indian's wrist. The movement was so smooth, it was almost as if the two of them had rehearsed it, as if the Indian had been trying to arc his wrist into the old man's grip. And the old man was twisting now, his foot out, catching the Indian by one ankle, pulling the leg from under him, the Indian going down all the time the old man twisted. He twisted so much that the Indian had to roll to ease the strain. Then the knife was falling, and the Indian was scrambling to his feet as the old man yanked the Indian toward him, toppling him again, jerking up his knee to meet the Indian's falling face. The force of the knee cracked the Indian's head up. His eyes rolled for a moment, blood flowing from his nose and mouth, as he fell past the knee, and the old man let him go then, let him hit, his hand lunging toward the Indian's throat, gripping, lifting. Until that moment Prentice had never realized how huge and strong the old man really was, the way he pulled the Indian completely off the ground, his facial muscles knotted from the effort, hoisting him, heaving him up one-handed until it was like the Indian was standing except that his feet were off the ground and he was hanging, feet dangling, as the old man hurtled forward with him, crashing him against a rock, spreading him across it so he couldn't move, still squeezing at his throat. The Indian's eyes were bulging. They didn't have a focus. And the old man kept squeezing, breathing heavily, squeezing.

It took that long for everyone to move, so caught up in things that only now were they responding, shouting for the old man to ease off, rushing toward him, grabbing at him. The old man kept squeezing. It was like he had been rooted to the spot. They pushed and pulled at him. They tried to pry his fingers free, but nothing worked.

"God dammit, stop!" one man shouted, and the voice brought Prentice to himself. He had been sitting, staring wide-eyed at the old man as he held the Indian high above his head, one hand around his throat, and let him hang there, inches off the ground, twitching. When the voice brought him to himself, Prentice grew afraid, standing suddenly, running toward the old man, in spite of himself coming up behind and locking arms around the old man's chest. The old man's chest was so huge that Prentice almost couldn't make his hands meet. Then he did, gripping, squeezing.

All the time, he was afraid. At first he couldn't get the old man's chest to give. Then the old man let out air to take a breath, and as his muscles slackened, Prentice pulled in, preventing the old man from taking in much more air. The old man exhaled again, and Prentice squeezed a little tighter, and now the old man had trouble breathing. He was rasping, struggling hard to shake Prentice off. The rest of the men were pulling at the old man's arm, prying at his hand. Prentice had the sense of people nearby shouting. The old man breathed, and Prentice squeezed a little tighter, and the old man wavered, thrashing, hunching, rasping, as he suddenly let go of the Indian's throat, sweeping with his good arm, scattering. Some troopers fell. Others stumbled back. Prentice still had hold of him, letting go, dropping to the ground. From where he lay, he looked up at the old man standing there, Calendar's arm outstretched, his hand open, his fingers clawed, glancing angrily all around at them, his big chest heaving, his eyes almost red, and the effect was that he wasn't human any longer, more like some ancient cornered bear, or a giant fending off the puny mortals after him, and the old man stood there, his face wild, staring all around at them, and suddenly he said, "Don't touch me. Touch me once again, I'll kill you."

The old man didn't speak to anyone in particular. Prentice wasn't even sure the old man knew who had gone against him. But Prentice couldn't help but be afraid, of what had nearly happened, of how the old man had behaved, of how the old man would react when he found that Prentice had gone against him, and abruptly Prentice felt sorry for him too, wanting to stand up and tell him, "Look, I'm sorry," but the old man was already moving away from them, sweeping through them, walking quite a distance. The rest of the men were rushing toward the Indian, slapping his back, lifting him to make him breathe, and the Indian made a sound low in his throat and rasped, his color coming back, marks across his throat, and they knew that he was going to be all right. They eased him to the ground, propping him against a rock, and in a moment he was moaning, nodding, his eyelids flicking. Someone went to get the surgeon. They were gesturing, talking about what had happened, looking toward the old man who was walking off along the base of the ridge. Nobody could figure what the point was. Prentice lay in the dust, afraid, finally stood and brushed the dust off, listened some more, glanced in the direction the old man had taken, made his choice, and started toward him.

▣▣▣▣▣ 60 ▣▣▣▣▣

"Look, I'm sorry."

The old man didn't seem to hear him. He was quite a distance from the camp, in among some boulders, braced against one, looking at the sunset. His side was to Prentice, his face in profile against the blue-orange sky, and his cheek muscles were still rigid, his lips pursed, his eyes aglare.

Prentice waited for a response, stepped a little closer, and waited again. He took a breath. "I said I'm sorry."

The old man waved at him disgustedly. "What for? You did me a favor."

"You understand? I was afraid you wouldn't."

"Sure. If I'd killed the bastard, I would have been up

155

on charges. Let him live. Even as it is, there'll be some trouble.''

"Wait a minute. You think that's why I helped?"

The old man turned to him, snapping. "No, that isn't why you helped. You did it because you didn't want me killing him, because the whole idea of it bothered you and you figured as soon as it was over and I came back to myself, I'd feel the same. Well, that's not how I feel at all. I'd just as soon have killed him. And I'd have slept sweeter because of it.''

"But why? I don't get it. What was he doing to you?"

"Standing there.''

"That's all?" Prentice shook his head and frowned. "You've had some trouble with him, he stood too close, so you tried to kill him.''

"No, I haven't had trouble with him. I haven't had anything to do with him. I don't want to have anything to do with him, and I expect him to feel the same. He shouldn't have come up next to me.''

"Well, I still don't get it.''

"I'm not asking you to. It doesn't make a difference to me whether you justify what I did. I'm not after your approval.''

Prentice stepped a little closer. "It's got nothing to do with approval. I'm just trying to understand you.''

"Don't even try. I told you before, you don't understand a thing.''

"Something to do with Apaches. You fought against them once, and now you still don't like them.''

"No, that's wrong. I fought Sioux and Cheyenne.''

"Well, then, that doesn't make any sense either.''

"Sure it does. Of course it does. What the hell's the matter with you? He's an Indian."

Prentice stared at him.

"What do you think this whole damn business is about? Do you think once you go up against somebody you restrict yourself to the ones against you carrying guns? It's the whole damn bunch of them. Somewhere, I don't care how far removed in his family, that Indian had a relative who was killed by a white man. He looks old enough that he just might have been there to see it himself. And he remembers. Just like those Mexicans we killed the other day have relatives and *they'll* remember. Just like people in the Civil War remember. And I don't want that Indian around me. I don't want that Indian even halfway close to me."

"You mean because you think he'd do something to you?"

"No, God dammit, he obviously wouldn't try anything against me, not standing there in full view like that. He wouldn't try anything in private either, an Indian among whites, although he might think a lot about it. I'm damn sure he wouldn't help me if I got in trouble, though. I just don't want him near me. Is that so hard to figure out? Look, forty years ago I went up against them. I didn't do it halfway. I convinced myself that they were the lowest meanest creatures on God's great earth, and I set out to kill every one of them I could. I hated everything about them. The very mention of them set me raging. And I didn't forget all that and suddenly shake hands with them just because the shooting stopped. 'There, there, buddy, that's all right. It was just a difference of opinion, and we'll be friends.' It doesn't work like that. When you go up against somebody, you fix it in your mind that it's for keeps. It's the only way to win. And you don't forget it. That Indian makes me angry just to look at him. He insults me, coming close, I'll slit his guts out.''

Prentice felt it rising up in him.

"Yeah," the old man told him. "Yeah, that's right. Now you're getting it. What do you think we're doing down here anyway? Playing some game? We're not just after a bunch of bandits. It's the whole damn outfit. You look at some Mexican walking down the road, and you tell me whose side he's on. He's just talked to Villa five miles down the road, and now he's pointing us the other way. Five miles up the road he runs into federals, and maybe he plays up to them by telling them the right way. Or maybe he doesn't. It's no matter. He'd just as soon put a burr under our saddle and see the lot of us be kicked to death. There's no way you can trust him. Just keep thinking he's a greaser. That'll set you straight about him.''

Prentice shook his head in fierce bewilderment. "But if that's the way you feel, what's the point? I mean, what are you doing down here? Nothing good will come of it.''

"Of course not. Nothing's going to change. This just happens to be what I know. I do it well.''

"But Mexicans, Indians, by the time you're done you don't trust anyone, don't like them, don't want them near you. You don't have anyone.''

The old man looked sharply at him, cocked his head, and pointed. "There now. Maybe you're getting to understand after all.''

"Well, I can't be like that.''

"Maybe yes. Maybe no. We'll have to see.''

"No. I don't *want* to be like that."

"Then you've got no business being here. You start treating somebody you're up against like he's human, you're as good as dead."

They stared at each other.

Prentice waited a moment, then turned to go. Abruptly he turned back.

"Look, I realize what you're saying. I just can't bring myself to go that far. Can you see that?"

"Sure," the old man said. "Of course I can. But if that's the case, I've got nothing more to teach you."

Prentice thought about it. "Maybe so."

They stared at each other again. Prentice tried to figure what to say, didn't know, looked at the sun going down, looked at the old man, and this time, turning, he didn't stop.

61

"THE major says it's all right if you come with me," Calendar said.

Prentice kept riding with the column. Near noon on the next day, low-slung jagged mountains to the right, rolling desert far off every other way, yucca, cactus, mesquite, jimson weed, sun-bleached rocks and sand.

And dust. Always the dust. It seemed the heat had never been worse. Prentice took off his round-brimmed, high-peaked trooper's hat and wiped his head. He didn't know why. The air was so dry, he had so little water in him, he didn't even sweat. Mostly it just gave him something to do, turning to the old man, staring at him.

They had been avoiding each other since the night before. At least Prentice knew that he had been avoiding the old man anyhow, staying close among a group of men, sleeping near them, saddling his horse in company with them. From time to time he had looked across and seen the old man at the edge of camp, staying to himself, sitting by a fire, staring into the darkness. Morning, the old man had been there too, and it wasn't so much that Prentice disapproved of what the old man had told him. Indeed, he recognized the strange logic of what the old man had said. He just couldn't make himself behave according to it, and he ended feeling so naive and foolish that he couldn't manage to go over and feel comfortable with him. The troopers had eaten and prepared their horses and then mounted, and still Prentice had not let himself go near him, the old man meeting with his scouts and sending one to brief the Indians, riding on his own before the column, coming back three hours later. By then the troop had covered nearly twenty miles, and listening to the men close by him talking while they rode, Prentice had found out that there'd been some trouble with the Indian after all. Not much, but enough. The major had sent for Calendar late the night before and again in the morning, and both times there'd been words. Nobody knew what exactly had been said—each time the major had taken Calendar aside to talk with him. But voices had been raised, that much was sure, and once this morning somebody had seen the major shake a fist at Calendar. Prentice wondered what the old man thought of that. Somebody else had seen the major shortly after his last conversation with the old man, and the major's face had been red and he was snapping orders to his officers.

All the time he heard that, Prentice had seen the old man riding beside the major at the head of the column. Then the old man had swung around, coming down the column's flank, passing him, Prentice looking straight ahead. The next thing, he was conscious of the old man coming up beside him. He did his best to keep looking straight ahead. The old man waited and then told him it was all right for him to come with him.

"What for?"

"I just want to show you something."

Prentice didn't respond.

"Well, what's it going to be?" Calendar asked.

They rode a little longer.

"Suit yourself," the old man said. He nudged his horse and moved ahead. Prentice watched him go. He knew that he himself was being proud, that he was trying to maintain a show, proving he was independent, but the farther off the old man went, the more he wished that he had gone with him, and before he thought much more about it, he was riding up beside him.

The old man looked at him. "You're sure you want to come?"

Prentice shrugged. "It beats eating dust."

"It does at that," the old man said.

Then the old man smiled. Not much of a smile, his teeth barely showing, his eyes not quite glittering, but all the same it was a smile, and this was the first time Prentice had ever seen him do it, and the smile had its effect. The

pride and tension drained from him. They angled from the
column, riding toward the distance, the old man leading,
Prentice feeling grateful, easier.

They rode for several hours. The old man stopped them
as they peaked a rise, the column out of sight behind them.
Off in front of them, the old man pointed toward the rows
of dips and ridges, rocks and cactus studding them, and
told him, "There."

"What?"

"It's simple. Find me water."

"I don't know anything about it."

"Just use common sense."

Prentice looked at him and saw that the old man wasn't
kidding. He took a breath and looked out at the desert
again. Then, exhaling, leaning forward in his saddle, he
set his mind to working. It made him nervous, the way the
old man was testing him. All the same there was a kind of
game to this, the joy of working out a puzzle, and while
just for a moment he was conscious of the old man staring
at him, he soon forgot himself and concentrated on the
problem.

"Well, let's see. Common sense. All right then, where
there's water, trees and bushes grow. I don't see any trees.
There's lots of bushes, mesquite really, but they're pretty
hardy and they're not in any pattern. It's for sure there
isn't water under every one of them. There's a clump of
them down in that arroyo a hundred yards to the right, but
my guess is that's from when the rains come. We might
find a sheltered pool down in there. I don't know. It's hard
to say. We'd have to look."

"Okay, that's fine. What else?"

"Animals, I suppose. If there was water, there'd be

animals. Likely small. A lizard maybe. A boar. A bird for all I know. When I think of animals instead of water, I notice something moving out there. Straight across. That moving dot between those ridges.''

"What kind do you think?"

"Too far to tell. Looks big enough to be a deer."

The old man reached back to his saddle bags and handed him binoculars.

Prentice focused on it. "My God."

"What is it?"

"A horse."

The old man clicked his tongue.

"You knew?"

"I just came back from there. That's what I want to show you."

Calendar took the glasses, slipped them in a saddle bag and buckled it, then grabbed his reins and started down the slope.

Getting to it took them quite a while, seeing it, losing sight of it, coming up over a ridge and catching sight of it again, getting closer all the time. At first it stayed a dot. Then the legs were clear, and the head, and the general proportions, and there wasn't any question what it was.

Prentice didn't understand. It didn't move as they got close. They were making enough noise that even if it didn't smell them it could hear them from quite a distance. It should have spooked. Either that or started toward them. Something one way or the other. But this horse didn't seem to pay them much attention. Then Prentice rode up and got a good look, and his stomach turned.

The horse had no eyes. Something had gouged them out so there were only runny sockets. The withers were worse, nothing but open sores where a saddle had been, white from pus and maggots dropping from it, green in spots where gangrene had set in. No wonder the horse hadn't spooked or been attracted to them. It had passed through pain, too numb to feel much of anything.

"My God, what happened to it?"

"Well, the saddle cuts are obvious. This is one of Villa's mounts. Not his personally, but you know what I mean. They rode it near to death, then left it here."

"But the eyes. What about the eyes?"

"That's the fancy part. It happened they found water near here, so they blinded it. That way the horse wouldn't wander too far from the water. Coming back, looking for the water, there was always the chance that they'd get their landmarks confused, but if they kept looking around, they had a good chance of seeing the horse. Like a road sign. Standard practice." And then he looked at him. "Nice people."

"Sure." Prentice was thinking of what the old man had told him the night before. "What about the water?"

"Right behind you."

Prentice turned, and there was a pool beneath a lip of rock.

"Not enough for the troop to bother with. We'll fill our canteens, water the horses, and head on back."

The old man slipped his semiautomatic from his holster.

"Wait a minute. What are you doing?"

"I'm going to shoot the horse."

"But you just said they'd be coming back this way. Shouldn't we leave it be, get the troop, and wait for them?"

"Not anymore. You can bet there's somebody watching us."

"What?"

"Not here," Calendar said. "Likely over there." He pointed toward the mountains. "Somebody up there with binoculars. That's standard practice too. If they know they're coming back this way, they'll leave somebody close-by to make sure the water hole's secure. Besides, this horse is going to drop pretty soon. From the look of those eyes—they've nearly stopped draining—it's been here a day or two. If they were planning to come back, they'd have done so long before now. They wouldn't take a chance on the horse dropping before they found the water again. No, any way you think of it, this hole is finished for us. Either somebody up there has seen us or they won't be coming back. There's no point in making the horse go through any more than it already has."

Calendar pulled the slide back on the pistol, chambering a cartridge, walked over to the horse, and aimed the pistol at a spot behind its ear.

He pulled the trigger, jerking from the recoil, a chunk of bone and flesh and brain bursting out the other side as the horse whipped down head first and landed with a snort, its legs out and shaking, then relaxed.

Calendar stood there looking down at it, the echo from the gunshot coming back, then turned. "Admit it. You already thought of that, but you kept yourself from doing it. That's right?"

Prentice nodded.

"Well, why didn't you?"

"Because I thought you'd say it was wrong."

"Now look. I know I come across as hard. But use your head. Provided it's practical, there's no reason to be cruel."

Prentice nodded again. "You're right. It's just that it's difficult to know when to do one thing and when to do another."

"You'll find out."

"I don't know. Sometimes I think I never will."

"Sure you will."

"I don't know." It occurred to Prentice that they were talking as if the conversation the night before had never happened, as if the lessons were still going on and he and the old man had not decided to cancel them.

But it didn't matter.

He looked at the old man and then at the horse, wishing that he'd had the confidence to speak up for what he thought was right, then shrugged numbly and told him, "Guess we'd better fill the canteens." They could bury the horse, he thought, reluctant even to suggest it; but that would take too long, and this way at least the vultures would have something. Anyway it wouldn't matter to the horse.

No, he thought, one way or another it wouldn't matter at all.

They filled their canteens, watered their mounts, looked around in case there was another pool nearby, eased up in their saddles, and rode back to the column. On the way Prentice asked the old man about other ways of finding water, learned about dry stream beds that still might have water in pockets under the sand, about mulching cactus and looking for animal paths and watching all day for flight patterns of birds. They stopped in the arroyo he had pointed out and checked around the mesquite clumps to see if there was water, but there wasn't. They got up in their saddles once again and continued to the column.

□□□□□ 62 □□□□□

THEY were being watched all right. Years later someone would piece together what had happened, going through old diaries and letters, talking to relatives of people who had been involved back then, and while some of the sources would contradict others, most were in agreement, and a few others that described subsequent incidents were compatible with them. Following Villa's wounding at Guerrero and his well-guarded retreat into the mountains, his band of one hundred and fifty men had begun to split up. This was no desertion, rather a calculated risk to keep attention from him. After all, his wagon had been ruined beyond repair when it slipped off the narrow road and tumbled down the mountainside. The procession had slowed, sixteen men carrying Villa on a litter while his horsemen led their mounts on foot behind him. It was just a matter of time before some of Pershing's soldiers found their trail—the string of horse feces would have been enough. That number of men traveling that slowly, it wouldn't take long for Pershing to catch up to them.

So they began disbanding, breaking off in groups of five and six, heading in all directions, sometimes stopped by Pershing's men and posing as Carranza sympathizers. Before they left, they all agreed to meet two months from then at the town of San Juan Bautista, in the province of

Durango. In the meantime, Villa's forces, reduced now to his litter bearers and three absolutely trusted friends, worked him farther through the mountains. They kept moving south, hoping eventually to get beyond the sweep of Pershing's search, descending briefly from the mountains to rest and get supplies, first at a hacienda, Cieneguita, and then at a town, Sierra del Oro, a little farther on.

But that tactic clearly wasn't one that they could count on. Ranches and small towns were the most obvious places that Pershing's soldiers would be looking for him, and while in better days Villa had depended on his lookouts to give him warning soon enough to get away, his wound now made him move too slowly for safety. It wasn't healing anyhow, black and festered, swollen. Villa was feverish, in pain, resting badly, delirious, afraid he was going to die. Either that or lose the leg. From all accounts, the stench was sickening, he and his men checking the wound each hour of the day for signs of gangrene. Helpless as he was, they had to get him to a safer place, finally deciding to take him back up to the mountains, hiding in the day, traveling at dawn and dusk and sometimes through the night until they got him high enough and found a likely cave.

It went in quite a distance, sheltered by brush, with a view of the desert far below and miles off on the other side a second range. There his litter bearers split into separate groups, moving off, leaving Villa with his three good friends, two men staying with him at all times, the third going down to spread the word that he was dead, to scout for news and come back on occasion with supplies. There his wound began to mend, the two friends with him dressing it with leaves from prickly pears, kneading stiffened muscles, helping him to stand a little and to hobble with a stick.

From there they kept watch on the desert floor. The dates are correct. Six days from Guerrero, April 3. The Thirteenth Cavalry passed that range just two days later, and one of Villa's friends would later say that shortly after they got settled in the cave, they had seen a column down there, several scouts riding ahead, two men stopping on a ridge down there and shooting what appeared to be an animal.

Calendar had been wrong about the horse. It wasn't one of Villa's, although the trick of blinding a horse near a water hole was one of Villa's tactics. It isn't certain who left the horse down there, although Calendar was right at least about their being watched. Even so, it wouldn't have mattered if the troop had kept guard on the water hole. One of the reasons Villa had stayed up in that particular cave was that there was a stream nearby. His men didn't need to go down to the desert for water. They just stayed up there and watched the column ride by and out of sight. Villa kept working with his leg, learning how to walk again. By April 3, the cold and dampness of the cave were getting to him, and they decided to go down to warm land. As a consequence, they wound up coming up against the Thirteenth one more time, and that contact, unimportant for Villa, was for Calendar and Prentice to make all the difference.

THREE

☐☐☐☐☐☐ 63 ☐☐☐☐☐☐

THREE whores came to camp. That was shortly after dark, and a sentry nearly shot them before he got the point. They were anywhere from thirty-five to fifty, stone-faced, droopy-breasted, their long hair braided, greasy, filmed with dust. They had a tall, thin, pencil-mustached pimp with them, in a suit that was a size too small, sleeves too short, jacket fully buttoned, seams stretched taut around his chest. He wore a bow tie on an angle and a battered watch that dangled from one buttonhole, and he kept smiling at the sentry all the time he neared him, his hat held in his hand, pointing toward the whores and jabbering about them. The sentry raised his rifle and told them all to stop. The light from the fires behind him showed them clearly, and he stared from them to the pimp and then back at them, and the pimp looked like an undertaker while the whores, who glanced sullenly around, seemed nothing more than random villagers he had taken up with, dressed in shapeless cotton gowns with brightly colored beads around their necks. All the same, the sentry shook his head and shouted for some help.

Two troopers got there first, and then the sergeant. The sergeant understood. He looked to find the major, saw that the major was walking away, thought he understood about that too, and made his choice. The men were ready for it, that was certain, talking more and more about it as the days wore on, sometimes breaking into fights, staring hard at peasant women, the women often running, lifting up their skirts, and scooping dirt within themselves to foil what they evidently thought was certain rape, the troopers angry at the insult, cursing them. They might not have been reduced enough to consider rape, but they understood that if it hadn't been for politics and an order forbidding them to fraternize they would have had access to the women and the liquor in the villages nearby, and with nothing to do, no relief for their boredom, their tempers were on edge. Strictly speaking, this was pandering to their weakness, and there didn't seem a reason to give in to them. All the same, the sergeant was fed up himself, and there didn't seem a reason not to give in either. As long as they were careful to avoid any kind of trap, as long as the major seemed inclined to turn the other way, the sergeant saw no harm in going through with it.

"That ring of boulders over there," he told the pimp. "No payment larger than five pesos or some food. An armed guard with you all the time."

The pimp, still grinning, seemed almost to curtsy. He faced the whores and harangued them, pointing toward the rocks. They shrugged and started toward them.

Then the sergeant turned, surprised that where before he'd had three troopers, now he had fifteen. Smiling to himself, deciding he would fix them for their eagerness, he told them, "Get your rifles. You can be the guard." They didn't balk. Indeed, they went off readily to get their rifles. They didn't mutter. That surprised him. Then he realized—they planned to watch.

Other troopers came now too, and he told them, "Don't bunch up." If the major was indeed deliberately looking the other way instead of just being busy, there wasn't any point in taking advantage of his pose. They'd have to keep this quiet, unobtrusive, or the major would think his pretense was a farce and put a stop to things.

That made sense, and the troopers spread the word. Before long, lots were drawn, and nearly everyone in camp was sitting by his bedroll, cleaning weapons, keeping busy, waiting for his turn.

The whores went in among the rocks, tugged up their skirts, and lay down beside each other. Three at a time the troopers went there, undid their pants, and settled to their knees upon them. In the darkness Prentice walked by Calendar and asked him, "Are you going?"

The old man, sitting with his back against a rock, looked up and shook his head. "I don't think much about that anymore." He struck a match and lit a cigarette. "Besides, I don't need pus hanging from my dick."

That stopped Prentice. "Do you think?"

"I *know*. If you've got a problem, beat it out." And then he smiled. "Just make sure you wash your hand. Sit down and save yourself some trouble."

Prentice looked at the ring of rocks by the edge of camp, looked at the old man sitting there, shrugged, and sat beside him.

Prentice didn't show it, but he felt relieved. He'd only

had relations with a woman once, and even then it hadn't been a woman but a girl, sixteen, the same as himself. It hadn't been intended, either. They had gotten to wrestling, then to kissing. One thing had simply led to another. He had ejaculated even as he entered, and she had called him names.

That had been in Ohio, near his father's farm. He'd been so awkward, and the girl had often had so many other boys around her that he hadn't gone around to her again, and anyway there hadn't been much time. The trouble with his father had started shortly after that.

His mother dead about a year by then, his father had tried very hard to work the farm and live without her. Then his health had failed. The city had tried to bring the farm within its limits, and the fight with the city had weakened his father even further. One day, driving a wagon full of rocks across a field and up a slope, he'd tried too sharp an angle. The wagon had tipped enough to dump him. The wagon had kept tipping, dropping the rocks on him, crushing him.

Prentice never knew what really had happened. The old man certainly knew better than to try that sharp an angle. It could be, weakened as he was, he had just forgotten himself. It could be too that the old man simply hadn't cared. Prentice never knew. He'd seen to the burial of his father, had seen the city take the land. It didn't matter. So much had happened there, his father and his mother, two brothers in their youth, he wouldn't have stayed regardless. He took the money that the city offered, a good deal less than what the land was worth, wandered for a while, debated what to do, finally put the money in a bank, and ended where he was.

Why he wasn't sure. Need for excitement, he pretended. That no doubt was some of it. A chance to learn, to be a part of something, to go places, see things, have a sense of order. Mostly, he suspected, he just wanted to be as far away from the sort of life his father had led as possible. A kind of penance, a working out of guilt: He should have stayed and fought to keep the land. The joke was that he had thought he'd end in Europe, and here he was in Mexico. All the same, he didn't know why early on he'd lied to Calendar, telling him that his father lived in an apartment in that city in Ohio.

He hadn't known how he would feel going to those women either, how he'd do it, the troopers standing guard and watching him. The mechanics of it was no problem, nor was the urge: On the trail, with nothing to do, he'd been thinking about women for some time. But the public nature of it, the idea of people watching him, of dirty sweated skin and dust and greasy clothes and the sperm of other men—he'd been put off by it, drawn only by the abstract need and by the other men who took it for granted that he'd be in on this.

Now, satisfied with a reason to refuse, preferring instead to spend the time with Calendar, he sat beside the old man, watching the troopers wait their turn, others coming back, and feeling relieved that he wouldn't have to go among those rocks, happy to be distanced from them, it was a moment before he realized that the old man had spoken to him.

"That's right," the old man said.

Prentice didn't understand.

"Tomorrow."

"What about tomorrow?"

177

"I'll be sixty-five."

Prentice didn't realize it, but he must have stared.

The old man looked at him. "What is it? Did you think it wouldn't come?"

"No. It's just that—"

"Just that what?"

Prentice shook his head. "I don't know what to say."

"Of course not. There isn't anything. It's just another day."

"Yes, but I suppose I ought to say congratulations anyway. I mean, I don't know how you feel. I don't know what to say."

"You don't know how I feel?" Calendar leaned back closer to the rock and, after puffing on his cigarette, exhaled slowly. "Well, let me put it this way. I'm no different now than ten or fifteen years ago. I've got a few more aches. I don't relieve myself as easily as I used to, I don't sleep as well, but I'm still as quick on my feet as ever, and my brain hasn't failed me any. At least I don't think it has. But the trouble is, a birthday like this, it reminds you." Calendar glanced off into the darkness and then looked back at Prentice. "It's like I can't overlook it anymore. I'm getting older."

It was the most introspective Prentice had ever heard him, one of the longest times he had ever heard the old man talk about himself—even considering their argument about the Indian, which hadn't been introspection so much as explanation. Plus it was the first time Prentice had ever heard the old man suggest any weakness in himself, and he couldn't get over it, just sat there looking at him.

"Do you want to hear a story?"

Prentice nodded, grateful for the chance to keep from speaking. "If you want to tell it."

"Oh, I want to tell it all right. It's about a birthday. Were you ever in Wyoming?"

Prentice shook his head. "Ohio and then here. A few stops in New York and Texas."

"Well, you'd like it. The northern part at least. The southern part's a lot like this, a little better maybe. Rocks and sand, sagebrush and scrub grass. A lot of nothing really. But the northern part is lovely. There's a string of mountains that stretch down from north to south. If you come in from the east, first you go through desert. Then you hit mountains, then desert, then mountains and desert and mountains again, and each range is different from the others, and each of them is lovely. Even the names are. The Bighorns, the Wind Rivers, the Tetons.

"I first went there in 1867, a year before Wyoming was a territory. There was a man with me in those days, and we worked as trail hands for a while. Then that business with the Indians got started, and we signed on with the cavalry. The man got killed—" Calendar thought a moment. "The main thing is, I put in five years with the cavalry, mostly down in Colorado, and I figured that was plenty, so I went up to Wyoming again and worked as a trail hand for another while, or any other kind of work I could find, got sick of that, and signed on with the cavalry again, this time as a scout.

"I knew Wyoming pretty well by then. The seventies were the worst time with the Indians, and I figured if I was going to be against them anyhow, I might as well be where I'd do some good. It took us quite a while. A lot of battles, mostly with the Sioux. But by 1880 we'd pretty much cleared them out.

"Then I didn't know what to do. I'd had enough of the cavalry. I didn't feel like riding trail, although that's what I wound up doing for a while. By the fall of 1880 I'd made a choice. One thing yet to do. Looking up at those mountains, captivated by them, you have no idea what working next to them all the time can do to you—fifty years too late, no chance of making any decent money from it, I bought a string of traps, supplies, a horse, a pack mule, started up, and damn near didn't make it through first snow.

"The Wind Rivers. I'd been up in them before, but usually with a herd and other men, and as soon as it looked like snow we left. Either that or with the cavalry, and then there was a lot of men, and if you needed help, you got it. But this was different. How much I didn't know. I'd managed to get a log hut up before the weather turned, but I hadn't thought far enough ahead about the horse and mule. I don't know what I must have been thinking of, that they'd be able to paw through the snow to get at the grass beneath, I'm just not sure. The snow came in the middle of October. In the night. Evidently rain first, then sleet, then snow, and when I came out in the morning, the horse and mule were dead. They hadn't froze to death. It was cold but not that cold. But they were caked with ice, especially on their faces, in and around the nose and mouth, and as near as I could tell, they'd suffocated.

"They were lying on their sides, almost covered by the snow, and it panicked me. You've got to remember that knowing what to do when you're with a bunch of people and knowing what to do on your own—there's a hell of a big difference between them. I stood there, the snow coming down around me, the horse and mule nearly covered by it, the wind picking up, clouds low, more snow coming, the air getting colder all the time, and I thought, My God, I'm going to die up here. Isn't that amazing? Everything I'd been through, and there I was, scared to death by a storm. I mean I really thought I was going to die. It was like somebody trying to smother me, and I wouldn't have felt that way if I hadn't been alone. I'm sure of it. If there'd been someone with me, I would just have said, 'Bad news,' and gone in to make some coffee and wait the storm out.

"But all I could think of was getting out of there. Get down to the lowlands. Coming up was wrong. As cocky as I'd been to come up on my own and now I couldn't wait to get away. I packed some food and dressed as warmly as I could and started out. There was a hunter's shack a half a day away and I figured I could make it there before the storm got worse, hole up for the night, and start down farther in the morning. I mean I really thought I could beat the storm.

"I set out, wading through the snow. It was deep, ten inches maybe, but not so deep that I couldn't walk, and I knew the trail that I'd come up on, a kind of draw that in the spring would be a stream bed, and I got to it and went down in, and the snow was deeper there, collecting in the wind and covering the rocks. I went a ways but finally couldn't make it, had to climb up out and try another route. Then the snow got thicker, and after a while I couldn't see much ahead of me, just vague shapes of trees and rocks, and in a mile or so the snow got thicker and I was in a whiteout. You know what that is? You ever been in one?''

Prentice shook his head.

"You can't tell land from sky. Everything's the same. The snow's so gray and thick around you, you can't see a tree right there in front of you. You can't hardly see your hand. Now you've got to remember that all this time my adrenaline was flowing, and if I was panicked before, I don't know how to describe what I went through next. Abject terror." Calendar laughed. "I didn't know which way I was going. I knew I'd never find the hunter's shack. I didn't even think I'd find the hut that I had made. But I knew it wasn't any use going forward, not that I knew which way that was, and I didn't see much point walking till I froze, and then, quick as that, something snapped, and I got control. Maybe I was just exhausted. The first excuse for shelter that I came to—a couple of boulders with a kind of hollow under them—I crawled in, scooped up the snow in front of me to form some kind of windbreak, and I waited. I knew enough that I shouldn't go to sleep, so I started eating to keep myself awake, and I figured the food would keep my body working anyhow, so I just sat in there, eating. Damn, I ate up nearly everything I'd taken with me, dried beef, biscuits, raisins, everything I had, and the snow kept piling up and the wind got worse, and I must have gone to sleep regardless because all of a sudden I couldn't breathe and I woke up, seeing nothing, snow on top of me, clawing to get out, and the sight of sun on snow was nearly blinding. I didn't know how long I'd been in there, a day at least, and I didn't know where I was or how I was going to move with the snow so deep, but this was clear: The hunter's shack was much too far. I'd have to go back to the hut I'd built. I was beginning to recognize a few shapes of peaks I knew, estimating where the hut was in relation to them, and it took me another day of pushing through the snow to get to it. As a matter of fact, after a few wrong turns, I found it fairly easily. The trick was pushing through the snow to get to it.

"Well, I slept for a day, and when I woke up, I understood some things. The first was how stupid I'd been, setting out that way. Hell, never mind setting out. Coming up on my own to start with. I didn't know the first damn thing about this. The second was that if I'd lived through what I'd done, I figured I could live through anything. The winter would be tougher than I'd thought, but if I kept my wits about me, it couldn't be much worse. I had a lot of food that I had left behind, too much to carry, and I knew that there'd be game around. Plus I had the horse and mule for extra meat, a kind of bonus when I thought about it— if I could ever get them thawed—and any way I looked at it things were better now.

"So I started in to trapping, just a little at a time, finding streams and lakes nearby that weren't too thick with ice, breaking through and wading in to bait the trap and set it, making sure to anchor it, soon finding tracks on land and spotting burrows, setting traps near them as well or near where bark was freshly stripped from bushes. Like everything else, I had a lot to learn of course. I'd had the traps explained to me, but hearing about it was quite a different thing from doing it, and sometimes I didn't set the bait well enough and the animal got clean away with it, or else be caught himself and took the trap as well or chewed his leg off. But gradually I did things better, anchored the traps better, set them better places, and before long I had beaver and fox and rabbit, sometimes wolf, and I skinned them right away and cooked the rabbit and the beaver and worked on the skins each night and saved the really fine work until the storms came.

"And they came often enough, but I was warm with lots of food and things to do, and I didn't really mind. I'd be up by sunrise, off all day and back by night, and the only real danger was getting frostbite from wading in the streams, but I had extra clothes along to change when I got wet, and this time I knew enough to try my snowshoes, and things weren't bad at all.

"For a time. But I didn't really know what winter was like until I waited through it up there. It went on and on, and the longer it got, the colder it got, and the snow got deeper, and I wouldn't have had any trouble going through one or two months, but then it was three and four. And five. And it seemed like it would never end. All of a sudden I found I was talking to myself, or to the animals I was skinning, or the trees, and the ice was so thick I couldn't break through it anymore, and the air was so cold that even the animals weren't coming out anymore, and I got to spending more and more days in the hut, getting up later, going to bed earlier, eating less, taking less care to wash myself or void myself, and all the time I went on talking to myself, going crazy for lack of someone else to talk to. It was as if I'd come full circle, from the initial panic of realizing I'd be all alone, to adjusting to it, to babbling to myself, alone again and in a lonely panic.

"Then a strange thing happened. I adjusted to that as well. I don't know how it happened. It wasn't exactly willpower. It was just that things somehow reduced themselves, got simpler. I'd proved that I didn't need the comforts. Now I didn't even need people. I found that for days on end it was enough for me just to sit by the fire, legs crossed, nothing in my head, seeing nothing, thinking nothing, hearing a kind of single tone that sounded on and on, and it was lovely. I never felt more relaxed or pure. The snow was above the hut by then and I had to dig an upward tunnel to get out, but I didn't go out much, just sat by the fire, and the weight of the snow around the cabin seemed to muffle me, and I suppose I would have stayed up there and died like that if it hadn't been for the thaw.

"The thaw came early that year. Or so they told me later. I had no way to tell if it was early or late. I finally didn't know what day or month it was or anything. But the thaw came early anyway, and it brought me back, slowly, me begrudging it. I really didn't want to fill my mind again. But it was like I didn't have any control over that either, and it brought me back.

"The cabin was soaked through with water anyhow, and I looked at the furs I had. Too many really. To get them down I'd have to pull them on a litter. But I'd caught them and it seemed like it would be a sin against the animals just to leave them, so I packed up what I needed and I packed the skins on the litter and I started. Because the snow was so deep it took me quite a while to reach that hunter's shack, and there were two cowboys there, and I hardly knew how to talk to them. Hell, they didn't know how to talk to me either. They took one look at me and they didn't know what to think. But they told me news. About the railroad. About the winter on the plain. I didn't want to hear it. It didn't mean a thing. And they told me what the day and month was, but I didn't want to hear that either, and it was only because of the hunter's shack that I'd come across them, and even though they offered help, I told them no and passed them quickly by.

"It took me several weeks to reach the nearest town. By then it was getting cold again, and the ground that had been wet was freezing, and it wasn't like being back in the hut. I found that I'd been spoiled again, that I needed comfort, that now I was actually looking forward to talking to people again, and I came out on this ridge and looked down at the town, the snow on the slopes thinning out and blending with the lowland, rocks and sagebrush and brown grass, and there'd been something nagging at me, something that I wasn't quite aware of but had something to do with what the cowboys had told me, something to do with the date, and then I realized. They'd said it was April second. That had been several weeks ago, and somewhere in between, on April ninth, I'd had my birthday. I couldn't get over it, that I was so out of myself I hadn't even remembered it, and thinking of that made me eager to get down and celebrate.

"And then I stopped myself. To this day I don't know why. Something about that good feeling I'd had back in the hut. Something about the independence I'd learned and managed in the winter. I'm not sure. All I knew, as sure as I'd ever been of anything, was that I wasn't going down just yet, that if I was going to celebrate my birthday I was going to do it where I'd lived so long—forever it seemed. And I stayed. I purified myself of thoughts of hot meals, of baths, a bed, a shave. My face was itchy, my body flecked with sores. I purified myself of thoughts of them as well. I went to sleep among the pelts and woke up in the morning and decided it was my birthday, and before I knew it, I assumed that cross-legged pose, and the tone came back, and the town was there below me but I didn't know it. Or much care. In time the feeling left me again, but that was two days later, and I went down to the town and everybody looked at me, and I sold the pelts and ate and soaked myself and got new clothes and slept in a bed, and before long I was corrupted again.

"But it didn't matter. I'd had that feeling, and although I've had it often since, it's never been the same and I've never been up in those mountains again—they wouldn't be the same either. But I think of that winter often, and especially that day I pretended was my birthday, as the best time of my life.

"In the spring of 1881.

"When I was thirty."

The old man had been looking into the darkness as he spoke, and now he turned, and Prentice didn't understand it, but the memory was obviously important to the old man, and he didn't know what to say. If that birthday back in 1881 was the best he'd ever had, the one tomorrow showed every sign that it would be among the worst, and Prentice didn't know what to do. He wanted to tell the old man that there wasn't any problem, that he still had lots of good years left, but Prentice knew it wasn't true. The old man didn't have much time. Not of the kind he wanted. The way of life he'd chosen, his body couldn't keep it up much longer. A year. Five years. Very soon he'd be no use. Prentice couldn't bring himself to tell him. So he sat there looking at the old man, sensing what was going on inside him, the old man peering into the darkness again, Prentice vaguely conscious of a shadow that came up beside him—"I've been trying to find you"—and the moment broke.

Prentice looked up slowly at the trooper standing there. "What is it?"

"What do you mean what is it? It's your turn."

"Oh, that. Well, take it for me."

"What? You must be kidding."

"Maybe. Take it for me anyway."

"You're sure?"

Prentice nodded.

"Well, all right."

And the trooper walked away. Prentice didn't even wait to see him go. He glanced back at the old man, but it wasn't any good now. The old man's face had changed, no longer open, no longer offering the chance for them to talk. So Prentice went on sitting there, peering into the darkness with the old man, and the troopers kept on waiting or coming back, and in a while there weren't so many of them waiting, and then there were none. Prentice looked at the old man, and the old man's eyes were closed, and Prentice thought that maybe he had gone to sleep. Standing quietly, Prentice reached for a blanket, covering him.

🞔🞔🞔🞔🞔 64 🞔🞔🞔🞔🞔

HE started drinking shortly after sunrise. At least that's how Prentice later figured it. He himself woke up a little afterward and saw that the old man was up and gone already. Prentice had been thinking about what to give the old man as a present and had finally decided, going to his saddle bags, taking out the tiny cloth-wrapped package, holding it and looking at it for a moment, then going off in search of him. He found him over by the livery wagons. The other men were making breakfast, packing up their gear, seeing to their horses, and Calendar had just fed and watered his, turning as the boy came up to him.

"Good morning."

The old man didn't answer. He had washed his face and shaved, the first time in many days. His shirt and pants were clean. His hair was combed, his hat held in his hand. He looked the finest, youngest he had so far seemed. He leaned against the wagon, shrugged, and smiled, and Prentice held the package toward him.

"You don't have a use for this, but it's the best thing I have."

The old man didn't understand. Then suddenly his eyes went strange. He straightened from the wagon, his forehead creasing, not so much in bother as surprise, and the next thing Prentice put the package in his hand.

The old man looked self-conscious. "I don't know what to say."

"There isn't any need. Just open it."

The old man paused and nodded. Then he paused again and putting down his hat he slipped away the twine, unwrapped the cloth, and peered down at the tiny cardboard box. He opened that and with his finger pushed away more cloth, then peered down at the shiny gold pocket watch.

He didn't move or blink or anything.

Prentice suddenly felt nervous. "It was a present from my father. The inscription seems to fit."

The old man stared at him. Then, his big hand taking

out the watch, he opened up the face, its catches snapping pleasantly, and Prentice thought of what the old man read, of how he himself had felt the day that he received it: *With affection on your birthday*.

The old man squinted at him.

"Just have a happy birthday."

"Sure." The old man nodded. Then he reached to shake hands with him, and that's when Prentice smelled it.

Actually he'd been smelling it for quite a while, but he had thought that it was something else, something rotten in the grain. Now the scent was unmistakable. His impulse was to mention it. Then he stopped himself, and even as he did, he found that he was saying it. "Have you been drinking?"

The old man looked at him. "That's just a little lotion after shaving."

Prentice shook his head.

"So what? I'm celebrating."

"I don't get it. Where have you been keeping it?"

"Oh, here and there. It's around if a person knows to ask about it. Don't tell me you want a little."

"No. My father didn't drink, and I don't either."

"Fundamentalist or something?"

"Something."

"Well, that's too bad. No, I take it back. That's good. Now there's more of it for me."

Prentice shook his head again.

"Don't tell me you thought I didn't drink."

"No. I guess I knew that."

"Well, what is it then? My drinking early in the morning?"

"I suppose."

"Well, let's see how you act when you get to sixty-five. Let's see if you don't take to drink yourself."

"That's no excuse."

"Oh, now listen to you. It's not a question of needing an excuse. It's a question of having fun. Come on, let's get your mind a little broader. You were set last night to go and see those girls, but now this morning you don't like it if I take a drink. There's a little contradiction there."

"Last night was different. Anyway I didn't go."

"But you were ready to. The point's not booze. It's me. Your father didn't drink, and you don't think that I should either. Well, I've got news for you. I'm not your father."

And that was that. A pleasant easy conversation had by various implications and wrong turns become another argument.

There wasn't any way to go ahead after what the old man had said. It was a kind of ultimatum, like a slap, and Prentice could either walk away or try to take the conversation backward.

It made him sick to see how badly things had gone.

"Hey, I don't want to talk to you like this. I just want to wish you happy birthday."

The old man stared at him.

"Really. I don't care about your drinking. I mean, what difference does it make? It doesn't really matter. Let's go back a little. Happy birthday."

The old man gradually relaxed. He shrugged. "I guess you're right."

"I'm sorry. It's my fault."

"No, I'm stubborn. It's a sign of age."

And Prentice had to smile. He knew he shouldn't, but he couldn't help it.

And the old man had to smile as well. "I think we'd best talk about something else."

Everything was going to be all right.

The old man looked down at the watch. "I'm grateful. You're right, I don't have any use for it, but I'm grateful anyhow, and I'll carry it with me just as if I used it. More than that, I'll value it. I can't recall a present I've enjoyed receiving more. Thank you."

Now everything was going to be all right for sure, and it was all Prentice could do to control himself and smile and nod.

Then the noise of the troopers getting ready was so insistent that they turned and looked, and Prentice said, "My God, I haven't even had a chance to feed my horse." He raised his hands in haste, shook his head and laughed, and hurried off. Behind him, standing by the wagon, he heard the old man laughing.

□□□□□ **65** □□□□□

THE laughter was hollow. For whatever reason, bothered by his birthday, determined not to let the boy's remarks about his drinking stop him, maybe just because he liked it, Calendar was drunk by noon.

He held it well at any rate. They'd gone twenty miles by then, traveling slowly while the scouts struck out to look for signs, and Calendar had come back, speaking to the major for a moment, then riding down and stopping by Prentice.

"Might as well come with me. Keep me from falling off my horse." Calendar said it low so no one else could hear.

Prentice looked at him. The old man had seemed fine to him, riding straight, everything deliberate. Maybe too deliberate. Now that he looked closer, the old man's face was red, his eyes a little unfocused, his hands unsteady on the saddle horn. The red on his face could be from the sun. The rest of it could be just from riding too long in the heat. But his speech was careful, his breath a little forced, and the way he sat straight up in the saddle was itself a little forced. If you put all that together and you knew that he'd been drinking, there wasn't any question: He was drunk.

Prentice shook his head. "Well, Jesus."

"What about it? Come on, let's go see some country."

And this time Prentice didn't even make an effort to hold back, although he wanted to. He'd been lying again. It wasn't that his father was a fundamentalist and didn't drink. His father wasn't much of anything, and he drank a lot. Toward the end at any rate. His wife dead, the city moving in on him, he'd taken more and more each day to drinking until he almost wasn't ever sober. That was what had killed him, not the rocks, although they had been what crushed him. He had gotten up drinking that day too. That was likely why he'd gone the wrong way up the slope, on an angle instead of directly up, because he had no thought; why he'd fallen instead of jumped and why instead of rolling he had lain there while the rocks came crushing down. Toward the last he'd gotten mean as well. No, not mean. On edge. He had needed to be humored, needed lots of care. Prentice had done both their jobs, cooked for him and washed his clothes and helped him to his bed. At first it was his father's due, then an obligation, and finally a chore. And after all that, his father had gone out stupidly and killed himself. It made him angry and a little sad.

Now he felt that way again, the old man riding stiffly ahead of him, Prentice coming up behind. That and disappointed. After all the old man had said about control, he turned out not to have it in himself. Now that Prentice thought about it, there were many things the old man did that didn't match the things he said—that business with the Indian, little things as well, things that Prentice wasn't even sure were wrong, like telling people too much how to do things, like taking it for granted he could come and go as he pleased, wearing moods and posturing. Maybe Prentice was wrong, but he was beginning to suspect that what he first had thought was respect that other people showed the old man was just tolerance and maybe even humor. He wondered if the old man was a parody, and suddenly he was embarrassed by him.

So much so that he didn't even want to stay and argue with him, just wanted to get the hell away from there. He imagined what the other troopers would be saying now that they were out of sight, the two of them angling down a sandy ridge, the old man reaching in his saddle bag and pulling out a whiskey bottle, the bottle three-fourths empty, drinking from it.

"Come on up here. What the hell's the matter with you?"

Prentice had been staying back deliberately, wanting to dissociate himself, but there wasn't any point in getting into an argument. What difference would it make? He would go along with this, let the old man have his way. The old man would keep at him if he didn't anyhow. When he got his chance, he would ride back to the column and work to keep the old man at a distance. In the meantime, nothing for it but to go along with this. No point in letting his emotions get the best of him.

So he rode up beside him and tried to look disinterested as the old man took another drink. Then the old man started talking, and Prentice did his best to be detached, but the old man had gone to the old days once again, and the spell began to work, and try as he might, Prentice found it hard to stay uninvolved.

1884, the old man told him. Kansas and Dodge City. How he'd left the mountains after that long winter, drifting south, working as a trail hand until he ended in the cattle towns. Abilene and Ellsworth, Wichita and Dodge, each of them had had its heyday, passing its importance to the next. 1884, one year before the drives to Kansas would be disallowed. But no one knew that then, and in spite of what the locals wanted, Dodge was quite an open town. The streets were lined up with the railroad, east to west, one half for the proper people, the other for the bars and hotels, gambling halls and brothels.

"They were pretty much the same. Every place could give you any action. Lots of gambling, drinks, and girls. Lots of fights as well. Nothing like you read about, guys standing in the streets and pulling guns. Mostly back-shooting, sometimes in the front. A fellow would open up a door and find his face blown off. The best place I remember was the Gold Room, a block down from the Long Branch, a kind of A-frame, sunlight showing through the cracks, but the icehouse was along the back and the best rooms were beside it. Sure, you'd have to rent a girl to get them. That was the way the pimp for that place competed with the others, but hot days the price was worth it, and sometimes it was just enough to sleep. The girls were something else. I remember once a hunter telling me how he went into one place and the first thing saw a guy pull out a gun, put it up against somebody's ear, and blow the man's head apart. One girl, sitting cross-legged on a table, jumped down, rubbed her hands in all the blood on the floor, then leaped up, crying, 'Cock-a-doodle-doo!' clapped her hands, and spattered blood all over herself. The hunter said he took one look and turned around and went back out of town. You can see why the locals kept complaining. They had a lot of money, but they weren't safe on the streets. A town of seven thousand would be twice that in peak season, not to mention all those cattle. Close to one hundred thousand cattle went through Dodge in just a couple of months. You can imagine what the noise was like, drovers coming in, all that trouble on the other side of town. They tried outlawing guns. They tried restricting barroom hours. Big-time sheriffs, heavy fines. Nothing seemed to work. You can see why they finally passed a law forbidding cattle coming in entirely. Of course, by then the big names were all gone. Earp and Holliday and Masterson, they all had troubles of their own, and anyway the signs were there for anyone to see. Dodge was growing up. In 1884 it had a roller skating rink. Hell, never mind the roller skating rink. It even had a water works and telephones. It wasn't going to put up with the cattle business too much longer.

"So I took up with some drovers heading south. I worked as a trail hand for a while in Texas. By 1885 I'd reached El Paso. There was a bar I liked. The Gem Saloon. And one night a couple of guys there got involved in the first real big-time civilian gunfight I ever saw. Wyatt Earp was there as well. The only time I ever saw him. He's important to the story, but not in the way you think. I was sitting in there when two cowhands came in and started drinking at the bar. They didn't need much. They were drunk when they came in. They'd had some trouble with a fellow down the street. The guy had slipped away, and now they'd set out looking for him. They had some trouble with the owner of the Gem, who wouldn't charge their drinks. Then they had some words with a faro dealer who was staring at them. Finally they split up, the one guy going to another bar while the other stayed around to see what he could find. There was a music hall you got to from the bar, and finally the guy that stayed went in and drew his gun and shouted, 'Where's that bastard who came in tonight?' Well, soldiers ducked, civilians panicked, the music stopped, dance-hall girls ran, and the guy just stood there with his gun out until he realized that the fellow he wanted wasn't there. He put away his gun, took off his hat, and bowed. 'Excuse me, everyone. Excuse me.' Then he smiled and turned and walked back out.

"That's when he saw Earp. Earp was sitting in a booth, and the other fellow recognized him. I hadn't known that Earp was there myself. Evidently no one had, but we all caught on real fast. The cowhand went over to him, tried to pick a fight. Earp was there to see a friend and didn't want this trouble, so he simply stood and showed he had no gun. Then he sat back down and said he wouldn't fight. He wasn't very tall or anything. His face was thin. He had this long wide drooping mustache and his hair slicked back, a fancy suit, a watch chain even, but he didn't blink. He had the hardest eyes I ever saw. He just kept staring at the man, and the man knew not to press it and backed down.

"Oh, the cowhand was smart all right, for all the good it did him. Because no sooner had he backed off than he turned and saw this fellow in a fancy suit at the bar. The fancy suit had been grinning. Then he caught himself, but not in time. The cowhand went over to him and tried to pick a fight, but the fancy suit had no gun, and so the cowhand kept abusing him. He finally got tired, went over to a corner where there was a billiard game, and stood watching by the wall. The fancy suit saw that the cowhand wasn't looking his way, muttered that he'd had enough, and walked over to the faro dealer. I guess he thought the dealer would be sympathetic. After all, the dealer had been rousted by the fellow too. But when he asked the dealer for a gun, the dealer told him no. I remember what he said. 'Have no trouble—go on out.' He sounded like he didn't know the language well. Not Mexican. But European somehow. Anyway the fancy suit didn't like that. He went around the table, looking for a gun, and found one in a drawer. That was when the cowhand back in the corner looked his way and saw what he had done. He came out with his handgun drawn, but he was drunk, and the fancy suit knew what he was doing. He knelt and gripped the gun in both hands, and he shot the cowhand twice, once in the shoulder, another in the stomach, spinning him, so that the only shot the cowhand got off was at the billiard table before he lurched outside and evidently fell against a streetcar going by. They told me later that he died. The fancy suit dropped the gun and went out through the back.

"And that was that, we thought. We settled down to drinking. The owner started cleaning up. Then some man ran in saying that the other cowhand was coming back, the one who'd been there with the first guy at the start. The trouble is the other cowhand had gotten the story wrong. The way he'd heard, it wasn't the fancy suit but the faro dealer who had shot his friend. That made sense, seeing how they'd argued earlier. Now the friend was coming back to even things. Well, the faro dealer—I never saw a man so scared. He didn't know the first thing about guns. The gun was only in the drawer because the owner had put it there. He hadn't wanted any trouble. He didn't want to get involved, but he didn't have much choice. He didn't see how he could run. The cowhand would only follow him. He didn't see how he could stay. The cowhand would simply shoot him. He was game, though. I'll say that for him. He grabbed the gun the cowboy had dropped and tried to figure what to do, and that's when Earp stepped in. At first I thought Earp was going to take the gun and use it on the cowboy himself. I almost felt relieved. But that isn't what he did. I don't know why, but Earp started talking to this faro dealer, and I still recall exactly what he said. It was the most remarkable thing I ever heard anybody say, a whole course on gunfighting right there on the spot, not the way they write about it but the way it really was, and each sentence made its point.

" 'Don't give him a chance. He'll come shooting. Have your gun cocked, but don't pull until you're certain what you're shooting at. Aim for his belly, low. The gun'll throw up a bit, but if you hold it tight and wait until he's close enough, you can't miss. Keep cool and take your time.'

"The cowboy came through the door, and Earp stepped back quickly. The dealer begged the cowboy to stop. The cowboy came forward, shooting. You could see the bullets hit the wall. And the dealer held the gun and waited. Lord, he waited until I couldn't figure how the other guy could miss. The cowboy kept coming until he was almost on top of him, and then the dealer aimed the gun and fired and shot him twice, the last one in the heart. I never saw a thing to beat it. The dealer turned to Earp and thanked him, and Earp just sat and smiled. The last I heard, the dealer left town and took up with the fancy suit someplace."

And on the old man went, drinking, riding, telling stories. He had finished his bottle quite a while before, throwing it away, and leaning back to reach inside his saddle bag, he pulled out another. Somehow, even throwing the empty bottle away seemed sloppy. At least he didn't shoot it, Prentice thought. He'd been afraid that as the old man threw it he would draw his gun and shoot it, and that would just have been too much. Booze and guns and letting people in the area know that he was near. But then the old man went on talking, and the magic started again, and Prentice found that he couldn't break away from it. The old man was going through each major detail of his life, arranging them until the pattern led up to this day. An examination of history, conscience, something, looking for some point, and Prentice found that he was taken by it. How after those mountains and that winter he had headed south to keep away from the cold, moving into Texas and then to Mexico, moving farther south until he almost reached the jungle, then turning back. It took him years. He looked for gold. He stopped in villages and helped the people work their land. He worked again with cattle.

"There's a town down there. Parral. I stayed there going down and coming back. Thirty years ago. Friendly, big. I wonder how it's changed. The major says we're going there. It's a kind of gateway to the south, and if Villa's anywhere around, the people there would know."

Calendar was slurring his words now, speaking slower, shorter, getting tired. He took another swallow from the bottle, reined back on his horse, and looked around.

"I've got to take a leak."

He said it with determination, as if that much was certain anyhow and he could say it well. He slipped from his horse. His left knee buckled, and he nearly fell. Then, standing straight, his chest stuck out, his eyes straight ahead, he pointed to a rock and started walking toward it. He veered a little getting there. He fumbled with his pants, reached in, and, after waiting, urinated on the rock. The rock turned dark with spray. He moved his pelvis, aiming toward the few remaining pale spots. Then just one was left, and the urine losing force, leading back to him and dribbling, Calendar tensed. One last tiny spray of urine turned the pale spot dark.

"There," he said and nodded, putting himself back in, fixing his pants. He turned and smiled, started back and fell.

Something cracked. He lay, tried to get up, and slumped down.

Prentice jumped from his horse and ran to him.

"Are you all right?" Prentice grabbed him underneath his arms. The old man's shirt was damp with sweat.

"I'm tired. I'll be fine."

Prentice helped him up.

"You're sure?"

"God dammit, I just said so, didn't I? I told you I'll be fine."

Prentice looked down at the rock the old man's chest had landed on.

The old man brushed his hands away. "I told you leave me be."

"You didn't tell me leave you be."

"Well, now I've told you."

"All right then!"

Prentice didn't need to take this. It didn't matter that he understood the reason. The old man, having fallen, was embarrassed, and now he had to compensate. His father had gotten that way too, and Prentice didn't need to take it.

Plus he understood the crack he had heard. It wasn't that he feared the old man's ribs were broken, although they might be, but he doubted it. The old man's chest had landed so the vest pocket where the watch was had cracked against the rock. Lifting him, Prentice had felt down where the watch was, hearing a faint metallic scrape and touching several moving parts. He didn't say a word. The old man knew. His eyes had changed when Prentice felt the watch. That was why he hadn't gotten up, not from stupor but from understanding what he'd done. And that was still another reason why he'd gotten so surly. He figured if he caused a fight he wouldn't have to face the problem.

They scowled at each other, both of them understanding what was going on, both angry, and they didn't speak the whole ride back, and they didn't speak about the watch, and Prentice never saw it again.

□□□□□ 66 □□□□□

"I want you to know we're grateful."

Prentice didn't understand.

The major led Prentice farther from the camp. "For what you're doing for him."

"The old man?"

"That's right."

So that was why the major had asked to see him and had led him off this way. Prentice couldn't believe it. After everything, the major was thanking him. He had to shake his head.

"I've never seen him take an interest like this before. Really. I appreciate it. He's not an easy man."

"That's not half of it."

The major couldn't help but smile. "I know it. Oh, but don't I know it. The thing is, the effort is worthwhile. There are certain kinds of people in the world, special people, that you have to make allowance for, and Calendar is one of them. He's got so much inside him, so many talents, so much that he's done and learned. We've been living off him quite a while, and now it's time he got a little in return."

DAVID MORRELL

Prentice didn't answer.

"I know that doesn't seem to match with him. You didn't see him in his prime. Hell, never mind his prime. Sixteen years ago in Cuba he stormed up a hill, troopers dropping all around him, toward a machine gun in a blockhouse. He had his rifle out in front of him, running, slipping in the long grass up that hill, and the machine gun kept firing and the troopers all around him kept falling, and he just kept running, leaving everyone behind, emptying his rifle, throwing it away, shooting with his handgun, the machine gun in front of him, running, dodging to one side, and he leaned in through the blockhouse window, shooting, emptying his handgun, taking out another, leaning in and shooting, and he killed more men than I had time to count, and when I talked to men about it later, they said his clothes were hanging on him by the stitching. Those machine-gun bullets had shot up one side of him and down the other, nicking him, scratching him, doing everything but hitting him, and his shirt and pants, you couldn't even start to count the holes. I want you to know that he's my friend. I don't care if he takes you from the column and goes off with you for what he says is teaching you. I don't care what he does. As long as it helps him, then it's fine."

"And what about his job? What about his job?"

The major looked at him. "Well, you don't need to worry. When the time comes, if there's trouble, you can bet that he'll do fine, just fine. You just watch and learn from him."

And the trouble was, Prentice knew the major was correct. The old man would be fine. Even at his worst, the old man was better than most people at their best. Regard-

204

less of their differences, Prentice still had lots to learn from him. From one point of view, if on his birthday he got drunk and sorry for himself, what difference did it make? The trouble was, there was another point of view, and Prentice didn't know what to do. He thought he had figured things. The old man was a nuisance. Best to stay away from him. Now he didn't know. He liked him and he didn't like him, and on top of everything, the major had come along and given him a public obligation.

67

"I think we'd better talk," Prentice said.

The old man was lying stretched out in a blanket, his head against his saddle, a distance from the other men. His eyes were closed when Prentice came up, but Prentice started talking anyhow, and the old man turned his head and looked at him.

For an awkward moment, neither spoke a word.

Prentice glanced down at the ground. He couldn't figure how to say it. "I've been lying to you."

The old man shrugged.

"I told you my father was living in an apartment in some city, but he's not. He's dead."

The old man shrugged again. "I know it."

Prentice didn't stop to ask. "I lied to you about another thing as well. Maybe not exactly lied, but I didn't contradict you either. You're right. I have been thinking of you as my father. In a way at least. You saved my life. I didn't know what I was doing, still don't, but now that I've been down here for a while, I know I'm not cut out for this. I've been using you as security. Somebody to talk to and protect me."

"That much was obvious from the start. What difference does it make?"

"The difference is that none of it is working. There are things about you I don't like. Half the time I'm disappointed in you. No, not that. Disgusted even. And the things you have to teach me don't seem important anymore. I'm just putting in my time. Once this is over I'll be gone. I've used you. Now I'm acting badly, and I feel ashamed. I wanted to explain, to tell you I'm sorry."

"Is that all? Are you through?"

"Just to tell you I won't be sucking off you anymore. We're close enough that we can't help but be together, but it won't be like before. If you don't act right, I won't stay around."

"Is that it now? You're sure?"

Prentice looked at him and nodded.

"Well, all right then, let me tell you something. I once had a wife and son. In 1897. El Paso. After I came back from Mexico."

Prentice couldn't help but stare.

"Sure," the old man said. "You didn't know that. Well, it's true. I've been staying away from the subject."

"What happened to them?"

"I don't know. She took the boy and went back east. A baby really, but I liked him well enough. He'd be just about your age right now, a little older maybe. You want someone to respect. I want someone who's devoted. We've been disappointing to each *other*.''

Prentice felt the tension drain from him. He'd been braced to talk this out, but now it didn't seem to matter. Nothing did. Before he realized, he had sat down on the ground, looking at his hands, then breathing deeply. ''So where does all that put us?''

''Nowhere. We've been thinking too much. Now we understand, and we don't like it. Maybe it would help if we were honest. Maybe if we stopped thinking of what each other could be and accepted what we are, maybe we'd still be friends.''

Prentice studied his hands again. This wasn't what he had expected. He'd thought it through, and he had decided. To make an honest break, then wait until this was over.

But the old man always had surprises for him. Just when he thought that he had figured things, the old man added something new, and then he was confused again. It had never occurred to him to wonder why the old man had agreed to help him. He had thought it was himself, not a special image that the old man had of him. It had never occurred to him that the old man had a special interest in him.

''Don't you ever want to see him?'' Prentice asked.

''Sure I do. She never told me where she went.''

''Why?''

''The baby wasn't mine. She'd had him by another man, a fellow I used to work with on trail drives. The guy got sick and died. I went around to see if I could help. The next thing, I proposed to her.''

The old man paused and rolled a cigarette.

''It was what you'd call a marriage of convenience. I'm

not kidding myself. I don't have anything special about myself that a woman might find attractive, excepting maybe strength. But she was close to twenty-five years younger than me, and she had a child, and there were a lot more men than women, most of them ready to take advantage. Well, I guess she was a little like yourself. She saw some security in me. And me. Well, I was damn near fifty. I'd been around, I'd done a lot, but I didn't have a thing to show for it. I looked at the child and got to thinking, and like I said, one day I was helping, the next day I proposed to her. She did her best. I can't take that away from her. She treated me about as good as any man could want. And I did my best too. I couldn't keep a wife and kid and live the way I had been. I took a job in town, clerking in a gunsmith's shop. When that got too much, I worked a long time on construction. But you know, it really wasn't what I needed. I didn't feel like keeping on the move, but all my life I'd lived outdoors, and she couldn't help but sense that a part of me was missing. I guess it really must have showed. I didn't mind. The way I felt, I would have gladly given anything, but it started wearing on me, took away my joy in things, and I guess that got her feeling guilty. After all, she didn't love me. We'd agreed on that much at the start. And young people, you know, they've got ambitions, energy, they like to do things, while I was happy just to come home tired after work and see that the bills were paid, see that she and the boy had lots of food and clothes and a decent shelter.

"One day she just told me she was leaving. I guess I understood. She'd needed help, she'd gotten it, and now she knew it wasn't going to work. It wasn't any good for me or her, she said. We talked about it. I'd do anything for her. I even paid their way to go. You can't imagine how I felt to see that boy go.''

''And she never told you where she went?''

Calendar shook his head. ''Looking through the window of the train as it pulled out was the last time I saw them. I often wonder how the boy turned out.''

''But what about her? How do you feel about her?''

''She was the nicest woman I ever knew. Not the most attractive, just the nicest. To this day I don't begrudge her. I often think about the boy, though. The whole thing took about a year. . . . After that I signed on with the Army. Then I was in Cuba.''

The change was so abrupt that Prentice didn't push the topic anymore. He waited, and the old man didn't speak. Prentice sat while the darkness settled. Then, putting out his hand, he told the old man, ''All right,'' and the old man looked at him and shook hands on it.

Prentice felt better than he had in quite a while.

68

AND it ended two days later, near Parral. They'd been riding hard, convinced that Villa was holed up there. It was logical—the gateway to the south. If Villa hadn't passed through already, he would be thinking of it. The fight at Guerrero, a more recent one at Agua Caliente, had cut his band in half and then in half again. The Thirteenth

had learned this information from prisoners the other troops had taken. If they kept pushing at him, Villa would have no choice but to head south and reorganize.

So they rode hard toward Parral and one day from it came across a farm. The place wasn't much. The major and the old man lay on a ridge and studied it. An adobe house that through their glasses looked just tall enough to have an upper story. A fallen wall, a crumbled roof, a veranda that was parched and listing. The major pointed at the broken lean-to for the horses, at the shattered gate to the corral. The old man nodded, studying the smaller buildings. There were two in back, a third a little to the right. Their doors were shut, their walls intact, in contrast with the house and stockpen.

"Could be. Could be not," the old man said. "It could be they just broke some things to make it look deserted."

So they made a choice and went in, a lieutenant and the old man taking one group down in back while the major waited until they had a chance to circle. When the major saw them moving in, he would start his own group down in front.

It took the old man's group an hour. God knows who had thought to build a farm there. God knows why as well. There wasn't anything the land would grow and nothing for the horses. Sand and rock and dry arroyos. Up and down and up and down some more. There wasn't even any cactus.

Two miles seemed to take forever. They started from the right, moving in an arc, riding slowly to keep the dust down, staying far enough away to keep from being spotted. Then they reined up opposite the ridge that they had started from and moved in toward the farm.

Prentice had a sense of being out of things. The blaze of the sun angling down on him, the barren yellow land, the monotonous up-and-down pattern of the arroyos, these had lulled him. He knew he should be more alert. He even felt a little nervous. But he couldn't help sensing that he was off somewhere and watching things. He looked with interest at the old man riding ahead, talking to the lieutenant: The old man was speaking softly, pointing as they rode a little nearer. The other men were riding slowly, looking to both sides, their bodies moving to the rhythm of their horses. Then they came to where some arroyos merged, leading toward the farm, and started down, and his sense of being out of things was even greater. The sloping walls obliterated the horizon. All Prentice saw on either side were rocks and sand and arroyos joining this one. A world unto themselves, riders moving slowly, horses clomping, traces jingling. Just them and the sky, the gully turning, turning again, growing deeper, wider, leading toward the farm, and Prentice went with it.

He hadn't had a chance to talk much with the old man since that night. They had been too busy, the old man scouting most of every day, coming back at night too tired to do much of anything but sleep. Even so, the few times they had talked were satisfying. It seemed to Prentice that the old man was more open, much less forced. Not that he talked very long or said too much of consequence. But his manner was more easy, as if he had passed through something bad inside him and now felt relieved.

Prentice felt the same. Now that he understood why he and the old man had acted as they had, he found that he was free of turmoil. He felt that he had grown somewhat, had adjusted to his needs and insecurities. He looked ahead at the old man, who was quiet now and studying the gully as it wound before them. It was good to see the old man working again. There wasn't any question: The old man knew what he was doing. There hadn't been a moment when he didn't seem in charge. He had slumped off for several days, but now he was at his best again, and maybe that was why Prentice felt so much out of this, riding with the column but a large part of him off somewhere— because the old man was controlling things.

They came around a bend, and the lieutenant was already lurching from his horse as the gunshot reached them. No one moved, just reined up, paralyzed and startled. Then two more shots came down on them, and everybody tumbled. They dove toward rocks and merging arroyos, the old man jumping from his horse and sprawling behind a mound of dirt. Prentice dove below a trough and couldn't keep from shaking. He saw that the old man was the first to draw his gun and fire. Two more shots came down, and the horses bolted, surging down the draw, and the dust they raised was great enough to give the old man cover as he scrambled toward the top.

Prentice looked down at his hand and saw his pistol. He couldn't figure when he'd drawn it. He watched the old man scramble up, took a breath, and scrambled toward him, other troopers scrambling with him. The ground gave way beneath him. He kneed and clawed and reached the top and stuck his head up, then jerked it back down, frightened. The land was far too open. After the enclosure of the arroyo, he couldn't stand things open. He crouched, trembling, just below the rim, the remaining troopers down there firing, the close walls of the arroyo magnifying their reports. The other troopers were crouched in a line behind him, and he was stunned to find that just as he was follow-ing the old man, they were following him. Looking ahead, he saw the old man slide up onto the rim, staying flat and crawling. Prentice grabbed the rim, slid up, stayed flat, and crawled after him. The gunshots were less loud now. He felt the sand and stones beneath him scratch his shirt and stomach. He tasted dust. He wiped his eyes to keep the sweat from stinging them.

Then the old man stopped. Prentice stopped as well, looking for the reason the old man waited. The arroyo turned near here and angled to the right, and they were almost to its edge. The old man waved his arm from back to front, and Prentice understood that the old man knew who was behind him. He heard movement in the arroyo.

The old man waved again, and Prentice crawled up next to him. The old man pointed to the right, and Prentice crawled in that direction. He stopped, ten feet between them, facing toward the arroyo's rim. Other troopers squirmed behind him. The old man nodded, drew his knees up, braced himself, and stood, shooting toward the gully. Prentice did the same. He got off four shots before he realized that the place was empty. He sensed the old man running past him, started running too, veered around the gully, fired again, emptied his gun, but still there wasn't anyone.

The old man kept running. Prentice hurried after him, fumbling to slide out the empty magazine, pushing in a fresh one, running more smoothly now as he caught up, and the gully angled right again, and this time there was movement. The old man was already firing as Prentice squeezed off three shots and saw the bodies dropping. There were six men down there, running with the gully, Mexicans, sombreros, bandoleers, baggy pants, rope-soled shoes, and rifles. Two of them had already fallen, another two now dropping. The last two dodged around another bend, and the old man bolted toward them, Prentice right behind. He saw them clearly. They were running madly down a straight part of the gully, and Prentice stopped to raise his pistol and aim and fire as the old man gripped his wrist and threw his aim off. Quite calmly the old man took a classic shooting stance, his body sideways, his right arm extended, the other held in back of him for balance as he fired twice and hit them both, one in the shoulder, the other in the leg. He let the recoil take him. Then he slowly let his arm down, studying the way they squirmed down there.

"I had no doubt that you could hit them, but I wanted them alive."

The old man didn't look at him, just kept staring down at them, but Prentice understood. The old man was already moving, heading toward the rim, easing down, starting toward them, his gun outstretched, his eyes never off them, careful.

"Check the other four. Make sure they're dead."

Prentice didn't need to think about it. He was already heading back. As quickly as that the fight was over. The whole thing hadn't lasted more than fifty seconds, but it had been the most intense experience that Prentice had ever been through. He was still excited when he reached the pocket where the two pair had been dropped. He had to control himself, think it through, do this right. Easing off the rim, he started toward them, keeping all of them in careful sight. He kicked away their rifles, then stepped back, checking them for any sign of movement. He saw which ones had their hands beneath their bodies. There were two, and he shot them in the head. Then he shot the other two as well, knowing somehow that this was how it had to be, even though he'd never seen it done before.

And then, satisfied, he slumped back. The shooting from the troopers in the draw had stopped. There were men up on the rim now, staring down at him. There were others walking toward him in the gully. They circled the bodies, staring at him, and he touched his cheek. It was burning. He didn't understand. Then he realized. He had been on the old man's right, and a shell, ejecting, had flipped out on him. He hadn't even noticed. He didn't care. He just kept sitting, rubbing his cheek, staring at the bodies, and he didn't know which ones were the old man's

215

and which were his, and he didn't care about that either, just kept sitting, rubbing his cheek, staring, the stomach-turning stench of open head and body wounds now reaching him. It may have been excitement, it may have been the stench, but suddenly his head was braced between his knees and he was heaving. It kept coming. It seemed he'd never get it out of him.

▣▣▣▣▣ 69 ▣▣▣▣▣

"You were wrong," Calendar said.

"You don't need to tell me. Dear God, I shot those four men in the head."

The old man frowned. "That isn't what I mean."

"Well, that's what *I* mean. Lord help me, I shot them. I didn't need to shoot them. They were dead. Anyone could tell it."

"Sure. Until you walked away, and one might have sat up and dropped you."

"There were other ways. I could have waited until I had help. Jesus Christ, I went down there alone to prove I could do it. Then I panicked, and I shot them. More than that, I liked it. I saw the way blood was flying from those heads, and I kept shooting. I hadn't had enough up on the top. I had to shoot four heads apart."

"You made sure no one else got hurt."

"That doesn't make a difference. Don't you understand? I don't like what I felt just then!"

"Now tell that to the men they killed. Ask the lieutenant in his grave if he thinks you should have done it."

"You still don't understand. I wasn't looking for revenge. I did it because I liked it!"

The old man frowned at him and pointed. "All right, listen. I've been patient with you. Now I'm telling you. Shape up. I don't care why you did it. You'll get over that. The fact is you made sure no one else got hurt.

"The other fact is you got careless. One magazine empty. Three more shots when we were chasing them. Four more when you checked those others. You were out of bullets, and you never thought to change the magazine again. Where the hell's your backup gun? You couldn't know if there were any more of them around. You left yourself wide open. That's what brooding gets you. Dead. Now I've got work to do. If I were you, I'd stop indulging myself and concentrate on how to stay alive. You don't have room for this."

The old man studied him a moment longer, then walked off, and Prentice watched him go. It was the first time that the old man had corrected him in this manner, not as a teacher or a father figure. This was truly different. He wasn't justifying or correcting out of principle but out of what seemed honest anger as he might have treated anyone whom he had finally lost his patience with. That was it— the old man wasn't posing anymore. He was acting as himself, and Prentice didn't know how he felt about that. He had lost and gained. He wasn't any longer special in the old man's eyes. Now he was a person, and he'd have to measure up.

Which he didn't think he could, and didn't care. Heads. He couldn't stop his hands from shaking, couldn't stop the feeling in his stomach. Heads. All he saw were heads exploding, flying bits of bone and brain and blood and hair.

□□□□□ 70 □□□□□

"HE says they own the place and saw some riders on the ridge," Calendar explained. "They panicked and ran out the back. Then they stumbled on to us. They panicked again and started shooting."

The major shook his head.

"I know," Calendar said. "I think he knows it too, but that's the best he can manage."

"And you're sure they're Villa's men?"

"No question of it. Their rifles have U.S. ARMY stamped across them, the same kind that were taken from Columbus. They panicked all right, but not because they thought we were raiders. They were running from Americans."

The major bit his lip and looked the other way. "So what about the other one?"

"I've asked him, but he doesn't want to answer. I'll give him one more chance."

Calendar turned to where the prisoner lay, shoulder blasted, bleeding onto the sand, and spoke to him in Spanish. The prisoner shook his head. The old man asked him once again, speaking slower as he mentioned Villa. The prisoner shook his head again.

The old man shrugged and turned to face the major. "What the hell, it was too much to expect. There are several kinds down here. One you start to question, they talk all day. The other has some kind of sense of honor. They figure they're as good as dead to start with, so they go out with a little style. Just our luck we got the second."

"So what do you suppose?"

"Well, we want to know where Villa is, and we figure he's nearby. I don't see how we have much choice. Leave them with me for a while."

"You don't see any other way?"

"Not unless we want to let them keep bleeding until they're crazy from the pain. That could take another day, and even then they might go stupid on us or just die."

The major rubbed his forehead. "Give them one more chance."

The old man spoke to them. The prisoners shook their heads. The major bit his lip and walked away.

🁢🁢🁢🁢🁢 71 🁢🁢🁢🁢🁢

"DEAR GOD," Prentice said. He had come up to the arroyo's edge, and looking down he saw the old man cutting on a Mexican. The prisoner was staked out naked, his privates showing, his body streaked with blood and slashes, writhing. His thigh was black and swollen from his gunshot wound, and the old man had the knife inside it, twisting.

The old man glanced up, startled. He was down on one knee, leaning on the other, working with the knife, and now he stopped and stared. "Someone get this kid out of here." He pointed to the men nearby him watching. Then he paused and turned and started working on the second prisoner. This man was staked out naked like the first, his body slashed the same, except that he was wounded in the shoulder, and the old man pushed the knife in there and twisted.

"That's right," Prentice said. "Someone get me out of here."

The others frowned up at him. No one made a move.

"Come on. I want someone to try."

Prentice drew his pistol.

"Please. I want someone to try."

But no one moved, and Prentice started climbing into the arroyo.

"You're damned right. You try to get me out of here, I'll blow your heads off. Stay away from me!"

Then he was at the bottom, walking toward the old man, who was still cutting.

"What's this about?" Prentice demanded.

The old man went on cutting.

Prentice stood behind him, waiting. "I'm asking you. Have you gone deaf or something? What the hell is this about?"

The old man gripped the knife so hard that his hand went white. He stood, and with the knife still in his hand, he turned and faced him. "I don't know what you think you're doing, but you've got no place here. Get away."

"Of course I've got a place here. You're my teacher, aren't you? Don't you think you ought to show me? Don't you think you ought to tell me what the hell you're doing?"

The old man didn't answer. Prentice walked past him, pointing toward the prisoners.

"How does this work anyhow? You start on one man, then get tired, and start on the other? That way the first man gets a chance to think about what you're doing to the second? Pain's not so much right now as what might happen next. Is that the way it works?"

The old man nodded. "Something like that."

"Sure. And just to keep it in the family you invite a crowd down here to watch."

Now Prentice was getting to it, not the fact of torture. He could understand that. A prisoner knew something that you needed, so you had to make him talk. In principle that was fine. But thinking it and seeing how it worked were two different things. Especially seeing this one. As he'd come up to the edge of the arroyo, the sickness not yet from his stomach, the first thing that had struck him was the silence, the disparity between what he saw and the way they were reacting, the old man down there cutting, the men nearby him watching, the prisoners staked out and writhing but not screaming, everybody quiet, not a whisper or a breath, no moans or anything. And the old man kneeling down there, cutting, twisting, probing, his head inclined, his elbow braced on one knee, involved and yet detached, looking so damned curious and relaxed, as if he were toying with some pattern in the sand or performing some experiment he had come to out of boredom and the results of which were finally not the point. But even that disparity wasn't what had done it. There was more. Looking from the old man cutting to the men nearby him watching, searching, looking for some shock or feeling or regret that this was how things had to be, Prentice had seen the Indian.

The Indian. The old man hadn't let only the men nearby him watch. He'd even let the Indian, and Prentice felt as if he'd seen a child molested or an altar fouled, as if he'd seen some unspeakable thing, and he wanted to tear the old man's eyes out, to grip his throat and crush it, to smash his brains and scatter them.

Heads. The image of those heads.

"That's right." Prentice whirled on him. "And you even let the Indian. And now I'm telling all of you. The show is over. Get away. And now I'm telling *you*. Don't come near me. You come near me again, so help me God I don't know what I'll do to you." He turned to face the others. "What's the holdup? Get away. Let the man enjoy his work." Prentice was raising his gun now, staring at them, and they frowned at him and one by one began to drift away, and then he turned and told Calendar, pointing, "You remember. Stay away." Barely able to restrain his rage, the sickness rising in him again, Prentice scrambled up the rise.

72

"Listen, you interfere like that again, you won't need to threaten me, I'll drop you," Calendar said.

He had found the boy as soon as he had finished, storming up the hill in search of him, catching sight of him in back of the corral where Prentice was digging graves. Two troopers spoke to Calendar as he raged toward the kid, but he didn't take in what they said. He just kept storming toward the figure digging graves, his footsteps landing heavily, kicking clumps of dirt and crushing mesquite, breathing hard and cursing, so the boy heard him coming and turned, his shovel raised, as Calendar charged up.

"I told you, get away!" the boy ordered. "I don't want you anywhere around."

"What's the matter with you?"

"What's the matter with *you*? Don't you get it yet? I saw your face, those buddies of yours watching. You were liking it!"

"Or maybe I just had to make it seem as if I did. Maybe I had to make those Mexicans believe I'd do anything to find out what I wanted."

"The difference is the same. God, you've been at this so long you can't tell the one thing from the other. You were liking it."

"It doesn't matter what you think. I found out what I wanted."

"You could have done it other ways."

"I doubt it. But that's not what's really getting to you. It's the Indian. I kept him there because I told them I was going to turn them over to him."

And now the boy was so angry that he raised the shovel as if to hit him, and the old man knew enough to back away.

"You were doing fine on your own," Prentice said. "You didn't need him. You just wanted to refine it. Lord, you think so much about the proper way to do things, you don't even understand your motives. You thought you were making a virtue of necessity when all the time you were glad to get the chance. You were *liking* it."

And now instead of hitting the old man, Prentice was suddenly digging the shovel into the sand and scooping dirt at him, again and again, dirt flying all over him, the old man feeling it in his eyes, his mouth, down his shirt, stumbling back, his hand up to shield himself, his head turned, the boy yelling, "Get the hell away! Hear me! Get away!" as the old man reached down for his gun, then thought better and backed off.

"All right," Calendar said. "All right! You feel that way about it, go on, dig your graves. And while you're at it, dig another. There's one prisoner dead back there. The other's not much better. And while you're at it, dig another one as well. The way you're going you're just as likely to end up in one too."

Then Calendar was turning, his shoulders hunched, walking away, brushing off dirt. This wasn't what he had expected. He'd come to dress the boy down, to show him what a fool he was, to get some sense in him, and now here he was walking away, feeling foolish, dirt all over him, his mouth dry and tasting dusty, feeling even a little embarrassed and he didn't know why, except that the kid had faced him down and he had lost, and dammit what was wrong with that kid anyhow?

73

"LISTEN, I want to explain."

Prentice turned his back on him. "Get the hell away."

74

"LISTEN, I—"

"Get away!"

▯▯▯▯▯ 75 ▯▯▯▯▯

A troop of Carranzista soldiers came to camp that night. The Thirteenth had stayed at the farm, using the sheds and farmhouse for protection, fixing the corral and putting horses in it, feeding them, and their campfires must have shown a long way off. The Carranzistas rode down to investigate. Stopped by sentries, learning that these were Americans, they had stayed back while their captain came to talk.

His name was Mesa, and while everyone was nervous, he did his best to make the Americans feel at ease. He couldn't have been friendlier. Too much so, it turned out, but they didn't realize until it was too late. Mesa sat beside a fire with the major. He explained how they were having trouble with Villistas, how they needed all the help they could get, how he would telephone to Parral and see that the Americans were welcomed. There was food and water, he told them, forage for the horses, a campsite and supplies. There even was a railroad they could use—and, looking at the major, he said that there was a club in town, Canadian he guessed. Mesa spent the night and ate there in the morning, mounted up and wished them all the best, saying he would go to a nearby town to telephone, and rode off to his troops. The soldiers felt relieved. Not because Mesa was gone, but because after having been

226

through so much, they thought they might actually get relief. Plus, the major hadn't let on, but the men whom Calendar had tortured had finally told them what they wanted. Villa was nearby. Likely in Parral or heading farther south. If the troop could get down to Parral and search the place, and, failing to find him there, hurry south to block the mountain passes to Durango, they could cut him off. That would leave him caught between the Thirteenth and the other columns heading south. With any luck, the chase was almost through.

So they mounted up and started toward Parral, and the old man, setting off to scout ahead, tried to get the boy to join him, but the boy just wasn't having any. Prentice told him, "Get away," again, and the old man rode ahead.

They reached better country, cactus, desert grass, and jimson, the ground less sandy, more like soil, the air a little cooler. They angled up from the desert, the mountains to their right, to their left a parched and rolling grassland, off ahead a sight they couldn't quite believe, green against the slightly rising ground, a line of trees.

The trees were cottonwood, and they almost camped beside them, but then seeing other trees a distance farther off, they moved their horses toward them, and the horses must have smelled it, working harder, faster, rushing toward it, surging to the stream, and the troopers had to force them back, taking off their saddles, walking them, cooling them, at last allowing them to drink—just a little—then a little more—then walking them some more.

It took several hours, and even then the horses hadn't had their fill. The soldiers strung a picket line and tied the horses underneath the trees. Then they ran down to the water, taking care of themselves. After that, they set to making camp, and in a while they let their horses drink a little more. Soon they had no choice. They had to make the horses quit. They couldn't let the horses eat now. All that water, the grain would make them sick, so the soldiers spread their rolls and cooked some food, and only just before they went to sleep did they give the horses anything to eat. Just a little, just enough to give them strength.

There'd been so much to do that the old man hadn't had a chance to talk with Prentice. Now he found the boy beside the stream, and, sitting in the darkness near him, he asked, "Can't we settle this another way?"

The boy just looked at him.

The old man continued sitting there, and in a while the boy got up to leave. "It isn't you," Prentice said. "It's everything." He walked away.

The old man couldn't understand it, couldn't make himself adjust to the way the boy abruptly shifted moods. He'd gotten so used to having the boy beside him. Now without him he felt incomplete.

Prentice understood it very well, and the old man wasn't really much to blame. He'd had all day to think about it, and he'd meant what he said. It wasn't the old man. It was everything. The whole damn thing. He hated it. The old man only represented it. He couldn't blame the old man if he went about the only thing he'd ever known. For him this thing was right. But not for Prentice. The things you had to do. The fights, the guns, the deprivation. And this godforsaken place. He'd never understood the word before. It was as if the country and the expedition had a blight upon them. Even now, near this stream, the trees beside him, the only reason he liked it was that it felt a little like being up north. He should have kept the farm, stayed and worked it, lived with the seasons, tended to his crops and watched them grow. Now he couldn't wait to get away, get back up there, start again, and do his best to make things grow.

Prentice looked back toward the old man, and he knew he ought to tell him. But he couldn't make himself. He'd trapped himself again. He'd made so big a thing of it that he couldn't swallow his pride. That and something else. The empty feeling in him that prevented him from doing much of anything. He simply couldn't make himself. He just wanted to be lulled, to sit back in his saddle, near that stream or by this tree, and let the time pass, wait to get away. He told himself that this was just a sinking feeling after action, that it was natural and would pass, but he knew it wasn't true. He'd taken pleasure. Then the spell had broken, and he had seen the heads that he had blown apart, the slashes on the men whom Calendar had tortured, smelled the stench of open bodies, and he'd understood. Now he couldn't bear himself, couldn't bear the old man, any of them, or the thing he was a part of, any of it, and he wanted it to end. He tried to find the blame and couldn't. They were down here for a reason, but then Villa had his reasons too. Calendar had his reasons. So did everyone. Prentice had the impression of circles within circles, and it seemed they never stopped. He just wanted to break through them, get away, deny them, but he knew he never would. That finally was what did it. That he knew he'd never break away, that as long as there were people there'd be reasons for killing, and all he wanted was to be alone. He looked at the old man, and all he felt was pity for him, and he knew that was the one thing he could never tell him.

So they journeyed to Parral. They fed their horses well that morning, knowing that once they got there they could get more grain. They fed themselves and saddled up and started off, thinking of good food and baths and something cold to drink, and sometime close to noon, the mountains ended to their right. A rolling plain stretched off before them, mostly cactus, here and there a cottonwood, some scrubbrush and some grass. They angled up a long and easy rise, and at the top they looked down and they saw it, the railway coming through from east to west, the rock walls and the trees, the adobe buildings golden brown in the sun. There looked to be five thousand buildings, bigger than Columbus, bigger than anything they had seen since coming into Mexico, and it spread and spread and spread, and for a moment there was the shock of coming out of the desert toward a town, and then they took the time to dust their clothes, tuck in shirts and straighten hats, and snap the flaps on their holsters lest they look like they were there for trouble.

They started down. The air got warmer as they neared. They wiped their sleeves across their sweaty faces, squinting toward the town, and they got closer, and after all, three hundred of them, you'd think that someone would have noticed, but no one came to greet them, so a hundred yards away the major made them stop. He took a hundred men and rode a little closer, stopping by a guardhouse at the railway station. For a moment the old man had the sense of being at Columbus. Then a guard came out and looked at them, and the old man knew that everything was wrong.

The major asked to see the chief of arms. The guard looked longer at them, then went off, and in a while came back, and, if anything, his eyes were even worse. The old man glanced around. He didn't like the feel of things. They had permission to go in, the guard was saying, and the old man didn't like that either. He didn't like the silence of the place, and riding across the tracks and down the main street of the town, seeing no one on the street, spotting faces peering out of doorways, children ducking out of sight, he had the sense of being in that town that he had first checked out when they had entered Mexico, and the only sound then too had been the clomp of horses' hooves on the hard-baked street, and he was feeling nervous just as he had then. Or maybe that was an afterthought. He hadn't really thought the town back there was wrong. He was just projecting onto it what had happened afterward, and maybe this place was just fine. And maybe not. He couldn't tell. It didn't matter anyhow. He was in it now, and he had no choice, he'd have to follow through.

The square had room enough for all of them. The major put them in a five-line-deep formation. He took the old man and five others and walked up to the office of the garrison. The place was like the other buildings, a little wider, but two-story like the rest, adobe-walled with support beams jutting from the roof. They waited for the man on guard to show them in. They waited quite a while. Then the major stepped up past him, and the old man and the others followed.

The man behind the desk just stared at them. He'd never heard of Mesa, wondered why on earth they'd stopped, and wished that they would get the hell away.

The old man felt his stomach turn. He realized too late that they'd been tricked, that Mesa was one of Villa's men.

Then, looking out the window, the old man saw people

coming toward the square, first from buildings to his right, next from side streets to his left, then from side streets straight across, women but no children, mostly men, and they knew so much what they were doing that they didn't even talk. The old man told the major what was going on. The major looked out too, and there were even more people crowding toward the square.

76

PRENTICE watched them come. He had seen the first man step around a corner, then three others, then many more. He glanced around and saw the others coming from all sides, and he reached down to unsnap the flap on his holster. Other troopers did the same. "Damn," he heard one say. They tensed, and Prentice didn't know about the others, but he prayed.

This was the first time he had seen a battle coming. The other times it had either come upon him so fast that he hadn't had a chance to think, or else as in that village farther north it had been at such a distance that he'd felt apart from it and had a chance to act. But this was different. This was right here, right now, coming toward him, and he had no time to act. He could see the glare of their brown eyes. Panic rising hotly in him, all he wanted was to break and rush away. He fought the urge, and as he did so, the way his hips were spread across the saddle, he felt his sphincter start to loosen. "No," he said, and something warm and wet squeezed out between his hips, and he wasn't scared now, he was mad. Looking to his left, he saw a mule-drawn cart, someone fooling with the mule as the mule went rigid, bolting toward the troop, and that was all he needed. He might not know what to do about all these people crowding toward him, but the mule he understood, adrenaline rushing through him, and he was grateful for the chance. He slipped his right leg up across the saddle horn, jumped to the ground, and moved out to face the mule. He wouldn't have tried it with a horse, but a mule slowed by a cart he thought he could manage, waiting until it was almost upon him, then stepping to one side and using all his force to lunge against its neck. He hit it with his shoulder, jolting it, grabbing at the reins and yanking down as he stuck one foot out and tripped it. The mule went down headfirst. It tangled in its harness, and the way it started braying, he feared that he had crippled it. But its legs looked good and it was jerking to get up, falling back, and he helped it up and knew it would be fine, straightening its traces, angling it another way and leaving it. Then he reached down for his pistol and turned to face the crowd. His shoulder ached, but it didn't matter. He was in it once again, and he felt good. He singled out the man who'd spooked the mule.

"Dammit, come on. Let's find out how you like it!"

Abruptly he heard a noise, and turning toward the garrison, he saw that the door was open, that the old man and the major and the others were coming out. There was a man in uniform in back of them, his jacket buttoned to his chin, dark-eyed, dark-faced, his mustache drooping past his lips, and the way he jerked his head from side to side it was obvious that he was scared. The major faced his troops as if to tell them something, but he never got the chance. Someone shouted at them. The major turned, and Prentice turned as well. A small man on an Appaloosa was riding through the square. He wore gray riding breeches and polished boots; he even had a riding crop; he had a Vandyke beard and an accent very strongly German. *"Viva!"* he shouted. *"Todos! Ahora! Viva Mexico!"* And the crowd began to move. The major shouted *"Viva Villa!"* back at him, and it came as such a shock that everybody had to laugh.

That might have done it, given them a chance to get away, but there was someone else behind the German, a woman who stood close to six feet tall, very heavy, carrying a Mauser, and if the German here was understandable, one of many agents sent to start a second front, the woman was a puzzle. She looked European but not German, somewhat Scandinavian, light-eyed, strong-faced, her hair combed back, and she was shouting at them with a perfect Spanish accent. Prentice didn't understand her, but the way she spat the words out made it clear that they were vile. She looked and sounded like she'd lived here many years, and what Prentice didn't know, or the old man, the major, or any of them, what didn't come out until much later, was that her name was Elisa Griensen, that she had sympathized with Villa for some time, that he was two doors down the street that she had come from. In her home. She was taking care of him, and maybe the villagers didn't know where he was either, but they looked as if they knew her and they started shouting with her that they wanted the Americans to go away. The officer from the garrison jerked his head some more and kept looking nervous. The crowd came closer and the major and the others hurried to their horses. Prentice mounted with them. "Let's get out of here!" the major said. They started from the square.

Someone shot behind him. Prentice wasn't sure, but it sounded too far back to be a trooper. Then he heard more shots, and, bullets zinging past his head, he ducked.

The old man was suddenly near him. "You stay close."

"Damned right I will."

And that was the old man's first mistake. He had gotten to smiling back there in the square, not from what the major shouted to the German but from how the boy had stopped that business with the mule. The boy had done all right. Indeed, he had been excellent. The Mexicans had stopped dead in their tracks when he faced them, and the old man didn't think he could have done it any better even if he'd tried himself. Whether from the training he had given him or the boy's own growing talent, the old man saw in him the makings of the very best, and he was drawn to him as he'd been drawn for several days, and he didn't want to let him out of sight.

They had their guns out as they galloped with the other troopers down the main street toward the outskirts, and there was other shooting from behind them and some now from the side streets, and the old man scanned the upper stories for any sign of rifle barrels sticking out of windows or of someone who might throw things down on them. Mostly he was making sure that no one touched the boy. He thought he saw a movement ahead, and he fired. Then they passed the window, and he scanned the other upper stories, the shooting now in back of him, as the major led them farther down the street. He looked ahead and saw the country open out, the outskirts dwindling, saw the railroad tracks, the guardhouse by the railroad station, saw the major lead them up the road across the tracks and angle to the left between two low-slung hills as the man on duty at the guardhouse came out aiming at them and the old man shot him, riding past. He looked across at where the major led them up between the low-slung hills, and once again he had the image of that draw in Colorado where they had come down to the river and been trapped by Indians. This time, though, it turned out that the draw was like the one outside the village farther north where they'd been chased by federals. Calendar came up through it, saw another basin, a hollow really, and it was even worse, the walls were too steep to get out, and they were trapped. They swung and started back. Charging out, the old man saw the Mexican soldiers mixed in with the villagers at the edge of town. He saw the Mexican soldiers mounting their horses. The major angled up the road that they had first come in on. The old man didn't understand that, why the major hadn't done that at the start, why he'd gone into that draw instead of racing straight ahead. Because the major didn't think they would be pursued? Because the major thought that things would quiet soon and everyone could talk? The old man didn't know, but he didn't think the major should have taken the chance. It didn't matter. They were riding in the open now, and the old man didn't need to worry much about the kid. The kid had done just fine, and when it came to horses, the kid did even better, riding hard and well, letting out his horse but not enough to tire it. The old man concentrated on himself, going through the shots he'd fired, counting how many he had left. He looked ahead and saw the other members of the troop.

They were up there on the road, milling in confusion, staring past them toward the town. He didn't understand why they had stayed, why they hadn't come to help, but they hadn't, and then the old man and the others reached them, and they stopped and turned, and the Mexican soldiers were all mounted now, charging toward them.

"Let's get out of here!" the major shouted again, and they didn't need to hear him. They turned as he spoke and raced along the road. The Mexican soldiers gained on them. They had fresher mounts, and they angled off on either side to try to flank the Americans. There were rock walls all across the fields, a series of them, fifty yards apart, straight off from the road. The Mexican soldiers back there hurtled the obstacles, coming faster, shooting. The old man looked ahead, and one platoon was pulling back as they were trained to do—to provide a delaying action. Calendar glanced beside him, and the boy was going with them. "No!" Calendar shouted, but the boy was with them now, dismounting. The old man wheeled his horse around and galloped back to him. He grabbed his rifle, jumped to the ground, and scrambled toward the boy behind the rock wall, bullets zinging past him.

"Dammit, what's the matter with you?"

But the boy wasn't hearing. He was firing with the others toward the Mexican soldiers.

And the old man had repeated his mistake. Pay attention to yourself, to what you're doing. It was a rule he'd broken only once before, saving Prentice's life back in Columbus. Even now he didn't realize that he was breaking it. Don't let anybody get to you. Concentrate on what you have to do. On his own he never would have stopped. He knew that this was stupid, that they needed better cover. But he couldn't keep from being with the boy. His sense of wrong was mixed with shock and fear and the instinct to protect him, and he didn't pay attention to it, firing with the boy across the rock wall toward the soldiers, bullets chipping all around him, troopers falling, soldiers falling out there too, and then the soldiers were too close, and he knew they'd have to go. He grabbed the boy and dragged him struggling backward. The other troopers were moving. They got on their horses, the old man shoving at the boy, and then they all were mounted, shooting backward as they galloped to rejoin the troop.

They never did. The Mexicans were gaining on them, riding down the fields, vaulting fences, either that or angling toward the road, and in a while the troopers had to stop again, jumping down and scrambling toward another wall, shooting over the top of it. This time the old man almost didn't stop—but he couldn't keep from staying with the boy, and now he was compounding things, ignoring easy targets, concentrating to protect the boy. He shot at anybody who aimed toward them, often pushed the boy down when their section of the wall drew heavy fire.

77

THE boy, for his part, didn't even notice. He was out of things, working the bolt on his Springfield, aiming, firing, working the bolt again, soldiers out there falling, and when he was pushed down or someone dragged him back, he only partly registered it, struggling toward the wall again, shooting, vaguely conscious of the other troopers rushing past him, someone shoving him against his horse, a part of him taking over as he mounted almost without knowing and galloped with the others down the road.

He'd never felt so out of things. No, that was wrong—so into things, so much involved with them. His rifle, his horse, the wall, the troopers and the soldiers, they were all together, bright and pure and clear, and he didn't know how far he galloped down the road, just knew that he was doing it and loving it, didn't know that he was stopping again, dismounting with the others, conscious only that he found himself against another wall, working the bolt again, firing, stopping to reload, conscious vaguely of a figure next to him, firing at some soldiers near him, leaning close to him, and then he pushed up, shooting again, and then he was reloading again, and on his horse again, and by a wall again, and then the sequence seemed to blur and happen all at once. Just for a moment a section of himself detached and looked at him, and he thought he had lost his mind.

78

THE old man never saw a thing to equal it, the way the boy was firing, sweat running down his face, dust mixed in with it, screaming, firing, soldiers out there dropping, troopers groaning, the boy still screaming in a kind of frenzy, and Calendar was in it with him, screaming, shooting, not even conscious that he was still protecting him as he took a bullet in his shoulder, the same place he had gotten hit when he'd fought those soldiers near that village farther north, and he was on his face. Even then the old man didn't know that he'd been hit until he tried to use that arm to brace himself and stand. The arm gave out, and he fell back. He squirmed onto his side and squinted at the arm. His sleeve was red and warm. The stain was spreading, but he felt no pain. Then the sound of the screaming, firing, brought him to himself, and he crawled to the wall. At least it was his left arm. At least he could still shoot. But when he knelt up, peering past the wall, he saw that the Mexican soldiers were too close, and he grabbed the boy again and dragged him toward his horse. He never knew where he got the strength and presence of mind to do so much at once, firing, shoving at the boy, getting him on his horse, wincing as he swung up on his own, the other troopers riding with him down the road.

They made three more stands like that, and there were hardly any troopers left, a few more coming back to join them, as they came to the top of a rise and saw a village far away, just a little one, but it was shelter, and he saw the column, tiny figures down there, digging in. But the Mexican soldiers were too close. The Americans couldn't take the chance of riding in the open all that way, so they leaped down one more time, stopping at the top, spreading out across the rise, diving behind boulders, into hollows, using anything for cover—they'd left the rock walls quite a ways behind—and the troopers in the village saw what they were doing, and mounted up to join them as the first wave hit the troopers on the rise. Even as it did, the old man running with the boy to get to cover found that the boy was gone. He turned and saw that the boy was flat out, blood across his face. At first he thought the boy had been hit. Then he saw the rock where he had landed, blood across it too, and understood that he had tripped. He ran to get him, dragging him to cover. The first wave hit them as they crouched behind a boulder, the old man shooting, levering his rifle, shooting. He dropped two soldiers as they neared the rise. The other troopers kept shooting as the first wave dropped back, joining with the others close behind.

The old man looked to see how badly the boy was hurt. The boy was blinking at him, blood across his cheek and hair. His eyes were back to normal. He was seeing the old man as if he hadn't noticed he was there before. "How long?" Prentice asked.

The old man frowned, and then he understood. How long had he been away. He tried to say "At least an hour"—more like two, but he had no way to know it—and he never got the chance to say it anyhow. The second wave was almost onto them. He nudged the boy and told him, "Grab your gun. You got me into this. Now finish it." And then he started shooting.

The boy had dropped his Springfield when he'd fallen. He drew his pistol, pulled the slide back, aimed, and started firing. The old man squeezed off two more shots, then his rifle clicked on empty. He drew his pistol, pulled the slide, and started firing. He dropped two soldiers. Then he saw another riding toward the boy, aimed, and dropped him as he took another bullet, this time in the side.

The boy was conscious of the old man as he fell. He looked and saw the old man writhing, aimed, and dropped the man who'd shot him, turned to see another riding toward him, aimed, and pulled the trigger, and when nothing happened, he knelt, feeling helpless as the soldier aimed and shot him, and a portion of his brain detached, and he was back on the farm, talking to the old man and his father. He knew that they'd be friends, and then the old man faded.

🁢🁢🁢🁢🁢 79 🁢🁢🁢🁢🁢

THE old man couldn't breathe. He tried to make his chest move, and it wouldn't. He felt his side on fire, his shoulder aching, as he fought to sit, and then a weight moved and he breathed. There were mounted troopers all around him, shooting along the rise, charging down there, and he couldn't move his legs. Then he saw a body flat across his thighs. It had slid down from his chest. He looked and saw the boy and moaned.

He struggled to get out from under. The boy was on his face. He turned him. He saw the head, and he was almost sick. Bone and blood and brain.

"Jesus," he told him. "Jesus."

"How long?" the boy was saying, blinking.

Calendar didn't understand how he could talk.

"Jesus, what happened to you? How'd you let this happen?"

Then Calendar saw the pistol in the boy's hand, the slide jammed back, the magazine empty.

"Your backup gun. I warned you about your backup gun. What's the matter with you? You wouldn't listen. Jesus." Calendar was crying now, and the boy was looking nowhere, his eyelids closing as he smiled.

Prentice muttered something, and the old man put his ear down to his lips. He asked him to repeat it.

"Wasn't good enough."

The old man, sobbing, didn't understand.

"Wasn't good enough. I wasn't a good enough student."

"No. It was me. I wasn't a good enough teacher."

But the boy just shook his head. Or tried to. Never finished.

And the old man sat and cradled him and cried.

□□□□□ **80** □□□□□

THEY talked about it later, how they found the old man sitting with the boy held in his arms, repeating, "I'm not good enough. Not good enough," as the troopers rode past him, shooting at the Mexican soldiers on the other side. He sat there crying. Then he gently set the boy down and stood and wiped the tears from his face, staring toward the soldiers riding down the other side.

His face went hard, his body into action, as if he hadn't been hit at all, let alone in the arm and in the side. He grabbed a rifle and began shooting at the Mexican soldiers. He emptied it and grabbed another and emptied it as well. Then he grabbed a fallen pistol, then another, cursing, lunging toward his horse, getting on it, riding toward the Mexican soldiers, and the troopers up there with him started after him, and if in that retreat the old man hadn't seen a thing to beat the frenzy of the kid, the troopers riding after him hadn't seen a thing to beat the old man either. They say he kept going, kicking at his horse until he was almost onto them, waiting until it seemed he couldn't miss, drawing one gun, aiming, shooting, using up its magazine, switching to the other, using up its magazine as well, sliding out the empty, slamming in a full, going on that way, aiming, firing, until he had no more magazines, switching to his shoulder gun, firing that as well, and they say that he killed more than thirty men that day—the count was never verified, but they all agreed that it was more than thirty—and the major, when he heard about it, wished that he had been there to see it. The major was reminded of the old man storming up that hill in Cuba, the old man riding fifty yards ahead of all the others, shooting at the Mexican soldiers, dropping them, as he took a bullet in the leg and then another in the shoulder, and that last one got him good and dropped him. He toppled sideways from the horse and landed face down in the dirt. Just as well, the major later said: The force was great enough, it stunned him, and he wasn't able to think about the boy. The troopers pulled up near him, shooting at the soldiers riding off. They jumped down, certain that the old man was dead. A miracle he wasn't. Maybe not. A man that big, determined, it was just his bad luck that he would live. They took him to the village, and the surgeon shook his head. But the surgeon did his best for him, and, hit four times, Calendar fooled them all and lived. Even so, it took him quite a while to come around—three days and a night—and even then he only looked at them and blinked. He didn't try to speak.

He lay in the village while the troopers waited out the siege. The Mexican soldiers had come back and encircled them on the hills. The major, having sent for help, had gotten relief near sunset on the first day of the siege. A band of Negro troopers had arrived in the village, and the major, overjoyed to see them, had yelled out that he could kiss the lot of them. A man named Young, the Negro officer in charge, had grinned at him and told him he could start on him right now.

But these extra troopers weren't enough, nor was a second Negro force that came in shortly after, and it wasn't until the fourth day of the siege, when a colonel and a major brought other forces into town, that the Mexican soldiers on the hills showed any signs of leaving. The troopers stayed another week. Then Pershing ordered them to head north. The old man was conscious by then, asking what had happened, avoiding any mention of the kid. He did see where the kid was buried, but he didn't say a word. They put the old man in a wagon, and, the major hated to admit it, the old man didn't argue, he was finished. They shipped him north, first to Colonia Dublán, then to Columbus, where everything had started.

81

CALENDAR came in on a wagon, and he barely knew the place. Tents stretched off in all directions, buildings stood where there had once been desert. He saw the new corrals and stables, the new bars and the barracks and the storage bins, several thousand troopers, at least a thousand work-men, M.P.s, armed policemen, thugs who kept watch on the workmen. More than that, he saw the airstrip and the motor pool, the aircraft-engine-testing site, motors sound-ing loudly all day long. People say he stayed there quite a while. Others say he left very soon. All agree that as soon as he could walk he wandered through the camp as if in search of familiar places.

82

THE Punitive Expedition never journeyed deeper than Par-ral. Having come so close to Villa and yet failed to catch him, it never got a better chance. Ordered by an angry Mexico that the expedition could go anywhere it wanted, except south or east or west, Pershing kept moving north. The country was too vast and wild, his command too spread out, his supply lines too extended. When in June another band of troopers fought against Carranzista forces, this time at a place called Carrizal, the outcry from Carranza was so strong that America and Mexico nearly went to war. The expedition found itself restricted even farther north and after that quite useless. Even so, it stayed another seven months. Pershing and a first lieutenant, George S. Patton, Jr., mindful of the war in Europe, worked out training methods that would be useful if the United States ever entered it—trenches, barbed wire, and machine guns—and when next year in April the United States did declare itself, Pershing's forces, two months back from Mexico, formed the core of U.S. forces overseas. Pershing was in charge of them, the A.E.F. they called it, America's Expeditionary Force, and just as Sheridan and Sherman had gone from the Civil War to fight the Indians, so Patton went from Mexico to World War I and then of course to France and World War II.

Villa, recovered from his wound, helped by people in Parral, went down to Durango and regrouped. He started hitting Carranzista outposts, first Satevó, Santa Isabel, Chihuahua City, then Parral, Torreón, Camargo, and half a dozen others. It looked as if he was a power once again. By then it didn't matter. He had served his purpose. His counterpart, Zapata, had been ambushed. Carranza, under rebel pressure, had grabbed all the wealth he could and fled, shot to death on his way to Veracruz. Obregón, once loyal to him, now himself a rebel, chose a puppet government and then himself took charge, shot to death some years later by a young man acting to protect the interests of the Catholic Church. In the meantime Villa had petitioned the government for a pardon and had been granted several thousand acres and a hacienda near Parral. There he lived for several years. In 1923, as a consequence of gambling debts and an argument over payment for some furniture he had taken, eight men waited for him in the upper story of a building in Parral. Villa drove by with six bodyguards—the car a Dodge, the kind that Pershing had led his expedition in—they fired so many times that no one should have had a chance. Somehow one man in the rear survived. They buried Villa in Parral. One year later someone opened up the grave and cut off his head. No one knows what happened to it. The car itself is in Chihuahua City, rusted, bullet riddled, encased in glass at the rear of a large pink house, now a museum, that was once Villa's home.

His last great battle was in 1919, in Juárez, across the border from El Paso, bullets hitting U.S. buildings, killing soldiers and civilians; and the commander of Fort Bliss, a man named Erwin who had been with Pershing down in Mexico, was so enraged that he directed his artillery to fire across the border toward a race track in Juárez where he could see that Villa's forces were holed up. Under cover of the shelling, a cavalry detachment crossed the Rio Grande, moving in on Villa's right flank. Negro soldiers, their rifles fixed with bayonets, crossed and moved in on the other flank. They put him thoroughly to rout, and, more than that, for the last time in its history, the U.S. cavalry put in a mounted pistol charge. There were many troopers in it who had been with Pershing down in Mexico, who had been with the Thirteenth and the major and the old man at Parral, and afterward as they retold that final charge there were many who would claim that they had seen the old man with them, fording with them across the Rio Grande into Mexico, converging on the race track, chasing Villa from the city. They would disagree on what Calendar looked like, what he wore, whether he seemed older or was slower, but they all agreed that they saw him, riding next to them, his shoulder holster where it always was, his pistol out and riding hard and shooting. And they all agreed on one more thing—that when their horses had run to their limit, when their ammunition was used up and they were forced to stop, the old man kept on going. Villa's forces angled up a ridge and over it, and the old man continued after them, a solitary speck against the midday sun, receding, angling up, a spot against the top, and he was gone.

DAVID MORRELL is the award-winning author of such acclaimed high-action thrillers as FIRST BLOOD, TESTAMENT, THE BROTHERHOOD OF THE ROSE, THE FIFTH PROFESSION, THE COVENANT OF THE FLAME, and ASSUMED IDENTITY. A former professor of American literature, he is also a graduate of the G. Gordon Liddy Academy of Corporate Security and an honorary lifetime member of the Special Operations Association. He lives in Santa Fe, New Mexico.